A KNIFE IN THE SKY

A KNIFE IN THE SKY

MARIE-CÉLIE AGNANT
TRANSLATED BY KATIA GRUBISIC

Toronto, Ontario, Canada
www.inanna.ca

Copyright © 2022 Katia Grubisic
Originally published in French by Les Éditions du remue-ménage as *Femmes au temps des carnassiers*, copyright © 2015 Marie-Célie Agnant.

Except for the use of short passages for review purposes, no part of this book may be reproduced, in part or in whole, or transmitted in any form or by any means, electronically or mechanically, including photocopying, recording, or any information or storage retrieval system, without prior permission in writing from the publisher or a licence from the Canadian Copyright Collective Agency (Access Copyright).

 Canada Council for the Arts / Conseil des Arts du Canada  ONTARIO ARTS COUNCIL CONSEIL DES ARTS DE L'ONTARIO an Ontario government agency un organisme du gouvernement de l'Ontario  Canadä

We gratefully acknowledge the support of the Canada Council for the Arts and the Ontario Arts Council for our publishing program. We also acknowledge the financial support of the Government of Canada.

Cover design: Val Fullard
Cover image: detail of mural portrait of Yvonne Hakim Rimpel, Port-au-Prince, commissioned by Fondation Devoir De Mémoire-Haïti, painting by Jerry Rosembert; photograph Fondation Devoir De Mémoire-Haïti.

Any references to historical events, real people, or real places are used fictitiously. Other names, characters, places and events are products of the author's imagination.

Every effort has been made to contact copyright holders; in the event of an error or omission, please notify the publisher.

Library and Archives Canada Cataloguing in Publication

Title: A knife in the sky / Marie-Célie Agnant ; translated by Katia Grubisic.
Other titles: Femmes au temps des carnassiers. English
Names: Agnant, Marie-Célie, author.
Description: Translation of: Femmes au temps des carnassiers .
Identifiers: Canadiana (print) 20220221510 | Canadiana (ebook) 20220221553 | ISBN 9781771339186 (softcover) | ISBN 9781771339193 (HTML) | ISBN 9781771339209 (PDF)
Classification: LCC PS8551.G62 F4513 2022 | DDC C843/.54—dc23

Printed and bound in Canada

Inanna Publications and Education Inc.
210 Founders College, York University
4700 Keele Street, Toronto, Ontario, Canada M3J 1P3
Telephone: (416) 736-5356 Fax: (416) 736-5765
Email: inanna.publications@inanna.ca   Website: www.inanna.ca

In memory of Yvonne Hakim Rimpel: No voice will ever be able to give her back her own, brutally suppressed on Sunday, January 5, 1958. This book is just to say that a story silenced is a story slaughtered.

CONTENTS

I

- 3 The Smell of Blood and Tar
- 22 Hatred in His Veins
- 30 As Night Falls
- 38 Raw October
- 44 Brigand's Ball in the Brothel of the Lord
- 53 Jeanne's Season of Sorrow
- 57 Béatrice Imbert
- 62 Women Dismantled
- 67 The Siege
- 71 Clarisse's Fury
- 75 One Last Time
- 85 The Attack

II

- 89 Granada, 1974
- 95 Poisoned Memory
- 99 What Life Remains
- 102 Stitches of Memory
- 110 Bitter Tongues
- 117 Forcing the Dawn
- 127 Children of Violence
- 133 Night-Blooming Cereus
- 139 Love, Relics, and Philosophy
- 146 As the Voiceless Cry
- 152 Marigot, a Shroud for a Caul

- 163 *Acknowledgements*
- 164 *Translator's Notes*

I

THE SMELL OF BLOOD AND TAR

B RONZE. THE NIGHTS ARE HARD AND COLD, made of bronze; that's the only word that comes to mind. We wander through the burnished dark, a burrow with no hope of daylight. Night in my head, in my limbs. The sky is brimming with long knives like sabres. The stars come out in clusters, gliding with a hiss, and let out a last breath before fizzling out on the ground. Every night, the sky is melting. And those knives—inscrutable, the sinister brilliance of the edge. How can I name the flood of molten metal inside me, the images from this dream that's no dream at all? The dawn, sallow or gleaming, cannot lift the shroud that cloaks the city, closing it in. Terror is a zealous jailer and each morning it springs at me, coils around my neck. It holds me, it reminds me that it's always there. The study where I've been hiding for three days is a cell. I spent the previous two nights, like the one now ending, on the floor, wedged between the wall and a tall mahogany cabinet.

I crawl out in a stupor. I'm beyond exhausted, I must look completely crazy. Barefoot and dazed, I inch toward the window. I look up but I can't see the open wounds in the vaulted sky, the blade's sharp gashes. Where have they gone, those rivulets of ink? All that ink, streaming from the weeping sky; in the night the heavens have emptied out, like a belly drained of blood. How can I be sure it was only a dream?

I'm doubting myself. I can't understand why no one is doing anything. Are we just supposed to accept that we're nothing now but caged animals?

I don't expect a miracle, but maybe the furor will pass; I wish the hatred would burn off, or maybe a wave will rise up, from the neighbourhoods, from every city—blind, mad anger unleashed—and its breath will carry them away, drag them out of the loathsome lairs where they hold court, and haul them to the gallows.

They are flesh eaters, hunters, butchers who've controlled our lives since the last elections, the tonton makout who keep watch in the night like alligators eyeing their prey. They're the ones who sent me the brown envelope. The message is a few typewritten words, six lines in red ink addressed to Madame Journalist. There's no way not to see the threat:

On avenue John Brown at the corner of Berne there was a newsstand run by an old man. He was stubborn. He'd been told many times that it would be better to sell candy or peanuts instead. He has been missing since yesterday. The good man will sell no more newspapers. And soon there will be no one to write them. Consider yourself warned.

My lips are quivering, frozen in a sour grin. I used to smile all the time, radiant and cheerful, but since all this started I don't smile much anymore. I found the envelope slipped under the fence and tore it open. The letter had neither a name nor a return address—unsurprisingly, there was no clue as to who the sender was. And who'll speak for that old man now? He'd been selling newspapers and old issues of magazines for years—yes, stubbornly. His death was mentioned in the newspaper, four paltry lines for the assassination of a retired Latin teacher who became a newsvendor. Found dead, bullet to the back of the neck. An investigation is under way, the article concluded laconically.

I stand up, leaning against the windowsill. At the top of the hill, I can see two cars, the infamous DKWs that are symbolic of the terror that's descended upon us. They're posted up there with their headlights off, at the second bend, under the flamboyant trees.

My anger rises; the presence at this ungodly hour of murderous vehicles near my home will not plunge me into despair, I swear. I can't deny the fear, but I will fight with all my strength not to let it paralyze me. Even the deadliest hurricanes eventually spend their strength. I try to convince myself. I have faced so much fear over the last few months, and I refuse to let myself be defeated by a new tool of repression.

The cars coast down the hill and disappear, the smell of death in their wake. There is no popular revolt, the wave doesn't come. The day is already well underway. A rooster crows, hoarse and sad.

◆

Get a hold of yourself, keep it together. The words go round and round in my head, I repeat them like a mantra, preaching to myself: *You have to finish the article, come on, you're making it easy for them, what they really want is to shut you up like all the others.*

I go back to my room, which I abandon every night to shelter in my study, because of the cabinet behind which I can take cover if the house comes under fire. It's not a great hiding spot, but maybe, with a bit of luck…I huddle in bed, seeking some softness under the covers, but I toss and turn, it's not working. My solitude, which I usually cherish, seems hostile. I'm so weary. It takes a superhuman effort not to give in to the onslaught of terror, that animal whose power I can barely see anymore behind the wall of silence that runs from north to south, east to west.

A bit before noon, I take a shower, and the cold water startles me awake. I slough at my skin with the harsh horsehair mitt. Anything to remind me that I'm alive, not some zonbi with no will of its own, a body with no soul locked up in a house that might become a tomb, or some docile beast bowing down to let itself be slaughtered without even trying to kick back. For the first time in my life, I regret not owning a gun. Desperate times call for desperate measures: Bé's words make me smile in spite of myself. Today, without hesitating for a second, I would unload a whole clip out the window. That's what I tell myself, but that's not how it works: they have a whole arsenal of horrors on their side, while I only have my words and my fear.

After I shower, I lock myself back in the study, determined to finish the article. The window is open a crack—I don't want to open it completely—and I hear the familiar little noises that mark my life, though it's no longer a life, only make-believe. For a second I let myself be lulled by the voices I hear. Judith and Steph live a few houses away from mine, but their words carry on the wind, the only thing that's still free in this country. They're singing the same song over and over, tirelessly—a swan song, the last verse of a fading childhood. Here we are, living in a time when the powers that be steal infants from their cradles, rip them from their mother's breast, toss them up in the air and catch them on the tip of bayonets. They've been forcing schoolchildren to attend executions. *Au clair de la lune…* Judith's voice trembles. *Ouvre-moi ta porte, je n'ai plus de feu.* My candle is out. All of six years old, almost seven, Steph berates his sister. "It's not like that, you're singing it backwards!" he shouts. "Do it again!" In the indolence of early afternoon, Steph's childish indignation turns into a giggle, and it irritates me. Now he's laughing at Judith's lisp. I set aside the article I've been working on for the past few days, on the old matter of land reform, and instead turn to the murder of the three young men whose bodies have just been found in Ganthier.

◆

The hours go by under a dull, heavy sky. A light rain falls, and daylight is gradually fading. I want to scream, to vomit the insufferable tension once and for all. The floor around me is strewn with newspapers and wads of paper. Another day gone, and I've written absolutely nothing. On a large sheet, I trace letters, fat and full. I scribble them in, over and over, until the tip of the pen pokes through, tearing the paper like meat to awaken the sleeping flesh of the indifferent notepad and make it scream so that something can finally be born. I write one sentence: *They have succeeded for one whole day in depriving me of speech.* During this lost day I've discovered how hard it is to cheat my body: I am so vulnerable. I'm shuddering, grinding my teeth. Frozen at my desk, my hands clenched on the armrests, I'm helpless. I can't even hear my nails scraping at the damask, I can't tame the terror gripping me.

In the dining room, the radio plays day and night in the background. Another broadcast is about to begin, the same steady stream of bad news. The announcer's words and his funereal tone seem both nearby and very far away, a voice spitting out the bilious perfume that has settled over the country. How long has it been since the—the coup, since Duvalier took power? All day long, it's the same, repeated, read and reread, relayed flatly by every station, because anyone who would dare engage in any semblance of critique or commentary over the airwaves would be crazy. I can't help but listen and it releases a clenched anger within me, outrage and dread distending like a cloud ready to burst. Razzias, assassinations, middle-of-the-night kidnappings, massacres…Are these heinous crimes commonplace now, warranting no debate or analysis? Must the whole country be in chains for someone to finally sound the alarm?

I promised myself I wouldn't go outside until I had finished my article. This is the third day I've been locked up in the house. I know I'm being watched.

The phone shrieks. I jump; the shrill sound in the empty house shatters my nerves. My heart leaps up in my throat, beating fast. A fly buzzes by and instead of the handset, I grab a long brown envelope and swat the insect as if it were my worst enemy. With a sharp thwack I swipe it down and crush it. I hate flies.

The phone rings again, more insistently this time, it seems. It's Bé again; she can come over, she says. She calls me morning and night, she offers to come clean the house or make me something to eat. "The avocado tree is absolutely keeling with fruit. And I bought you some star apples. Your favourites," she wheedles. She tells me about my sister, who keeps coming home after dark. "We can't afford to be reckless like that anymore," she says under her breath. We have the same conversation every day. "I need to be alone to write, Bé," I tell her, again. She won't have it. She doesn't understand how angry I am; my stomach, my whole body is full to the brim with futile anger. All I can manage is crackers and some fruit juice. She will come tomorrow, she warns me. "I'll be there, whatever it takes. I'll come early and I'll bring a nice giraumon to make you soup." Bé knows I can't resist her soup, it's like velvet against my sadness. I try to talk her out of it. "That's all we need now, for them to keep us from eating together!" she grumbles, and hangs up without letting me say another word.

Bé will come see to the house tomorrow. She will bring out the magic of the pots and pans, she'll try to bury rage and fear with the bright orange of the squash. There's nothing simpler, nothing more authentic.

And all of a sudden it's evening. Even today, I haven't seen the time go by, as if the day had swept without transition from dawn to dusk. The neighbours must have put their children to bed. The nursery rhymes have gone quiet, but my own chorus comes back. *Don't give in, don't give up.*

"In the commune of Ganthier, the bodies of three young people in their twenties were found by some local children at the dump. The bodies were severely mutilated, and will be impossible to restore," the radio bleats dully.

I've started typing again but my hands refuse to go on. My fingers stop, stiff with anger. I stand up abruptly and the chair tips over, taking the pedestal table with it, and the glass of water I'd just put down smashes on the ceramic floor. The broken glass, the crash—it's innocuous, really, but it's threatening to me. I hold back a scream and rush into the dining room. It's unbearable, the news never stops, sowing terror. I turn off the radio, go back to the study, and clean up the broken glass before getting back to work.

On a corner of the table, above a pile of newspapers waiting to be filed, the brown envelope is a reminder.

◆

I'm clanging away at my typewriter again. I have only one goal: just write it, finish the article before Bé gets here.

Are we condemned to be passive witnesses to this degradation? Here is a nation that must be rebuilt and yet it is breathing its last, debased by a suffocating terror. Today we live in a time of crimes committed without consequence, a time of death foretold, of manipulation. They lock us up in our own homes, choke us with the cries muffled in our innards, and so we bend.

Can I get my words to line up, to remind me that I am more than merely a stubborn woman macerating in dread? For a while, the ideas come, they flow, and I am fierce and intact. Then, slowly, gradually, nothing. The surge recedes. A whirlwind of sand grinds through the gears in my brain. Whole days I've been struggling with words and worry. Now my thoughts are loose, at odds. But I have to finish, I have to beat this, to win the duel. I get up, walk around, sit down, start typing again: I delete, pace back and forth, I'm dreaming of an explosion of words, for the anger to finally boil over, the rumbling inside me to burst out.

Another long night looms. The darkness spreads over everything. Outside, the trees cast shadows that blur into the silhouettes of the few people who are out on the street, rushing home. They didn't even need to impose a curfew, the curfew took hold by itself, a tacit, perverse agreement. There is a curfew in our brains, our gestures, in our furtive glances and hushed footsteps. I have to turn off the lights. Tonight, I follow the advice of Toni, my neighbour and an old friend of Bé's, and swap the crystal bobeche lamp for a candle, hoping the flame will be more discreet. I wedge myself against the big cabinet on a sleeping bag and a couple of pillows.

Later, I start awake. It's dark. I hear a piercing, high-pitched scream, and moans, and it rekindles an ancient hurt inside me. At the bottom of the hill a woman is curled up in the fetal position. Who can save her? There's no ambulance, no clinic, there are no doctors nearby. Only soldiers and militia. I fumble for matches and strike one, but the candle has burned down, there's only a small stub of hardened wax at the bottom of the plate, and there is that fear again, its leaden heart, clotted in our guts.

◆

At seven-thirty in the morning, Bé troops in with her vegetables— already peeled and cut into pieces, she announces in a high-pitched voice, as if to break the silence. May the giraumon take up the whole space, may it irradiate the house with its bright orange flesh. Bé puts down a plastic bag full of papaya-coloured cubes and takes me in her arms. I can hear her heart pounding. She must have seen the cars up on the road. They must have forced her out of her car and searched her. I don't bother asking, she wouldn't tell me anyway. Who is trying to protect whom? I spare Bé because of her old age; what is she protecting me from? She says she has to protect me from myself, which always throws me off. It feel so good to huddle against Bé's chest. I could almost go to sleep, just a few minutes more. I breathe in the smell of her skin, her hair, the same scent since childhood, the same Camay soap, but etched into the present—a smell from before the horror, before the disaster. What's Bé thinking about? She pulls away and, her voice faltering expectedly, declares: "It will be delicious!" Then she thrusts a metal pan under my nose, full of fresh vegetables: leeks, turnips, carrots, celery. The pungent scent of sorrel wafts through the kitchen. It reminds me of life. I try to get caught up in the game, but my anxiety catches up with me. Bé is barely speaking now, she's buzzing around the kitchen in small, busy steps. "Forget that I'm here, I won't stop you from working," she says in a tone that brooks no disagreement.

Back in the study, I hear the familiar tinkle of cups and spoons. The aroma of freshly ground coffee spreads throughout the house like an echo. Bé brings me a cup of coffee, brewed strong the way I like it. She holds her own cup with both hands, firmly, and I know she's trying to keep from shaking. Bé sits down in front of me. Her face is drawn. She put her makeup on in a hurry this morning, and the blush is redder on one side than the other. *Poor little Pierrot*, I think as I look at her. She looks tinier every day, wrinkled and forsaken. I drink the coffee, savouring each small sip gratefully. Bé's eyes meet mine and I try to look away, staring at the grounds in the bottom of the cup. I don't want to hear about safety again. Bé knows; she drains her coffee, gets up and tightens the apron sliding down over her shrinking hips, shrugs her shoulders, and goes back to her pots and pans.

A little while later, I hear her rummaging around in her purse, and coins clink on the tiles. She must have dropped her wallet. How long have I been sitting here with the cup in my hands? Bé comes back in. "Here," she says, triumphantly. "I thought I'd lost it." She unfolds a four-year-old newspaper clipping. It's about me: *Mika Pelrin is an exceptional and resolute woman devoted to journalism with an uncommon passion and an unequivocal commitment, in a country where the profession is too often confused with loyalty to the regime.* Those days seem so far away. I reread the sentences, which a colleague had written when I won a prize given out by the journalists' association.

"The commitment's still there, but the passion is worn down, Bé," I tell her. How can we keep the fire burning when journalism is nothing more than a trough with a herd of wild animals wading around, attracted by the waft of carrion oozing from power? In these debauched times, this era of every excess imaginable, the profession of journalist, for those who still practice it with any freedom or independence, looks more and more like a fight with a deadly outcome. Passion and commitment might more easily be dubbed recklessness, I know that. Isn't that how many people define me? What they should say, however, is much simpler: *Mika Pelrin, an ordinary citizen, who wants to live with her eyes open.* Is that why I see danger wherever I look? I ask Bé what she thinks. She grabs the cups and is heading back to the kitchen when she hears the door. It's Toni, who scratches three times, as she always does.

Bé told her she was coming over. She runs to her friend. Toni, with her secrets and her prayers—gossip, her dirt, as Bé calls it, and she doesn't even know the half of it.

As soon as she comes in, Toni starts right into a story about a fire that destroyed a beautiful church in Babiole. Dismayed, she tells us about the church of the Holy Martyrs—razed, top to bottom. Toni's daughter Clara was there, she saw it all on her way home from work yesterday. The authorities, Toni chatters on, had been accusing Father Quemener, the Breton priest who's lived on the island for over forty years, of harbouring kamoken, dissidents. At first, from the road, Clara couldn't see the flames, but she knew there was a fire: everything was surrounded by smoke, and you could smell the tang of aged pitch pine sweating out of the wood. Clara could hear the crowd—there must have been dozens of people there, and they were mad. As she drew closer, Clara heard a boom as the walls collapsed, and sparks sprayed high into the air. The blaze growled as it consumed everything, and flames rose in tongues toward the sky.

Bé and I are aghast, silent. The whole country will soon be nothing but ruins and lament.

The interior of the carved-stone church was made of huruasa and the parquet floor of sand boramalli, precious woods brought over from Guyana. The parishioners were so proud, and people came from all over the country to see the stained glass windows that capped the three naves, worked by a craftsman trained by the master glaziers Lassus and Didron. The church was considered a jewel of the architectural heritage of the Caribbean. It was without a doubt one of the oldest and most imposing churches in the country.

A stately cactus hedge had been planted around the building, the trunks covered with long, sharp thorns—to guard the church, people said. These fascinating plants, a rare species native to Madagascar, bloomed twice a year, festooned in enormous fuchsia flowers.

Father Quemener had apparently fled the day before, knowing that neither his prayers nor the cacti guaranteed any protection.

"I couldn't help it, I needed to be there. I had to see with my own eyes what was left of the church after such a sacrilege," Toni goes on.

Bé interrupts. "What? Don't tell me you went over there?"

"Early this morning, I went over. I couldn't resist. I went for a walk with Clara, while I was at it," Toni explains. "It's an utter calamity!"

Toni lifts her arms to the sky in despair. She pulls a wide, crumpled handkerchief from her pocket and blows her nose noisily. "It's impossible not to weep: whole sections of walls have caved in, charred statues are scattered among the rubble. And all those cacti—ashes."

With quivering lips, she sniffs. "What did we do? Bé, did we trespass against heaven to have to live through such horrors? All those trunks lined up with their blackened thorns, their branches like sooty fists raised furiously to the sky. It reminded me of the skeleton of some prehistoric monster," she says tragically, a sob in her voice.

For once, Bé is speechless. She looks at Toni, worried. As she listens to her friend, she must be thinking that the world is falling apart at such blistering speed that it surely has to end soon. Toni's voice cracks and her muffled sobs sink into me. I am haunted. There's so much sorrow in that voice: how many of us on this island are choking back our sobs?

◆

Defiantly, at noon we sit on the terrace to eat. Bé puts out a linen tablecloth and crystal glasses. The soft green of the lemonade, the embroidered placemats, the flowers—two fleshy hibiscus in a glass—everything reminds us that love and beauty still exist. "Will you do us the honour of having some soup, Mimi? I go one week without seeing you and already you're nothing but skin and bones." I smile. She shakes her head. "It's no good," she says, discouraged. "It's no good, and your smile doesn't fool me."

Bé's outdone herself, and the intoxicating smell of her soup, the tickle of leaves in the warm midday air…This is life, and it should make people happy. Bé sighs after each bite. "It's rare that I get to eat after I cook," Bé apologizes. "You know that, Mimi."

I don't answer, but I know it's not true. Soup joumou is her favourite. I force myself to finish my plate. Toni, who usually eats more than her fill, barely touches her food.

At the end of the meal, Bé announces that Jean-François will be coming to pick her up and take her home.

"Did I tell you, Mimi? It was him who brought me this morning. I would have taken too long in a camionette. He's a good boy," she says again, "hard-working, and he's always so polite." She pulls her chair closer.

"I forgot to tell you, Mika. He told me his father was tired of being unemployed: he's a blue and red bandit now, he's joined up with the Volunteers of the National Security." *There goes another one.*

"You didn't know?" Toni breaks in. Her silence was beginning to worry me.

Bé jumps and tells her to lower her voice.

"Another one of Lafontant's recruits!" Toni squawks again.

Bé looks around, worried. Toni forges on: "Lafontant is a bastard. They say he's the one who's been operating in Montagne Noire. Cocky as all get out to have traded his medical books for the guns Duvalier is handing out. Surely you've heard of him, Mika?"

I nod. "He's not the only one who's given in. That's the tragedy."

"If there is any justice in this world," Toni mumbles, "they will be punished. They will have to be severely punished for their sins against this country."

She crosses herself. Bé stares at her, and starts eating again without enthusiasm before sliding her plate away. Toni looks at her friend apologetically. Her face falls, as if Bé's grief has gone right through her.

"Here," she says after a second, "relax a little, Béa darling. Let me tell you a story: yet another episode in the adventures of my brother Apollo."

"Him again?"

"The very same. My baby brother, I've only got one. And I will call him Apollo until I die, because he's as handsome as a monkey's ass," Toni says.

"Which doesn't stop him from collecting mistresses," Bé interjects, "but let's get to the story."

"Apollo," Toni begins, "is in the hospital at Saint Francis de Sales, courtesy of Zaza."

"What do you mean, courtesy of Zaza?"

Toni watches as a glimmer of amusement dances in her friend's eyes. Encouraged, she goes on: "Less than a week ago, our dear Zaza welcomed Apollo at the bakery with a hail of eggs."

"A hail of eggs?" Bé laughs.

"What I said, my friend. Eggs happen to be quite a weapon, according to Zaza. There's nothing like eggs, for the shock and the knock-down. Zaza couldn't stop laughing. She told me all about it. So Apollo comes to the bakery, arrogant as ever, to check the till. And as if that wasn't enough, he starts sniffing around, asking questions. Some customers haven't paid their tabs, so he threatens Zaza."

"The revenues did not meet the expectations of the self-proclaimed supervisor?"

"I'm getting there," Toni says, waving at Bé to be quiet. "As it happens, Zaza wasn't quite her usually agreeable self that day. Like a woman possessed, she grabs a basket of eggs she'd just bought to make her cakes, and bam, bam, bam! Apollo didn't even have time to duck, and Zaza barely stopped to take a breath. In the blink of an eye, Apollo was done and undone! Our dear commander goes down, flat on his back. Broken femur, no less."

"It's like I always say," Bé hoots, "you've got to know how to use the weapons you've got!"

Toni's story ends in a concert of chuckles. She's laughing so hard she starts to cough. Between hiccups, Bé insists, "You don't think there's something else going on?"

"Oh, Zaza has a long list of grievances against Apollo," Toni replies, wiping her eyes. "Monsieur is arrogant as heck. It's not enough for him to live off the proceeds of the bakery without getting his hands dirty. One thing's for sure, Bé: not every hunter is wise. They're too sure of themselves, they forget that even prey have their day. Though between you and me, Apollo's broken femur is the least of my troubles."

The two of them are laughing so hard they're crying. I leave them to their guffaws and gossip, and I go lie down. When I get up from my nap an hour later, Toni's gone and Bé is ready to head out too, with Jean-François. He greets me when he arrives, polite. He stands at the door to my study, his eyes wide at the clutter of books on my shelves. The kids are starving for knowledge, and all we have to offer are weapons. He's so young and already so discouraged, disillusioned.

He offers me his services—to do my shopping, he says, or he can drive me, even at night, if I have to go out for an emergency. "It's safer. People are just overwhelmed, they're terrified. And God knows they're right," he whispers, infinite sadness in his eyes.

◆

With Bé here and Toni's chatter, the day flew by again. After they leave, I tidy up the kitchen. It's hard to come back to reality; the house is quieter than ever. Even the chatty bird that's been yawping all afternoon in the branches of the almond tree deprives me of its trills now as evening falls. All the same, Bé's visit did me good. I go back to work with a little more spirit.

We know that nothing will stop the jackals who claim to run the country. Have we already forgotten that in less than two weeks in Ganthier alone more than forty people have been killed, and many more injured? The whole country should have anticipated what recent months have confirmed. These mass killings had been announced even before the butchers moved into the palace. Thousands of deaths in Bel-Air, Saint-Martin, La Saline and other working-class neighbourhoods paved the road to power before the elections, but somehow that's all in the past: people believe we must forget in order to survive, but we all know that is impossible. These latest events, with the army and the militia firing into a crowd of students, and now the recent discovery of more bodies, leave no doubt: there is no limit to the carnage. Let us never forget the vile words of the editor of the state newspaper the day after the attack on the students: "The parents of these scatterbrained youth should have taught them to respect authority. Now all they have left is to mourn their dead."

How many impotent tears will we shed? Again this morning, crippled by fear, we all listened to the radio stations counting new victims in Bainet, Jacmel, Saltrou, Plaisance, and Cazale. Some residents had the unpleasant surprise of waking up to crosses traced on their doors in blood and tar. It is no secret that five torture chambers have been set up in the basement of the presidential palace, with the most sophisticated equipment, along with those in the Dessalines Barracks and the National Penitentiary. The Father of the Nation, as he calls himself, the Supreme Guide, the Revolutionary, the Apostle of National Unity, the Most Worthy Heir of the Founders of the Fatherland, has been able to keep his stranglehold. Very quickly, to the satisfaction of the masters of the universe in the international community, he was able to subdue the unruly, lock up a host of opponents, assassinate thousands of dissenters, and exile hundreds of citizens. Today he is being rewarded with new weapons.

The installation of these "workrooms"—that is the euphemism they use—is possible in large part thanks to the boundless generosity *of the government of the United States of America, with the on-the-ground support of Nazi has-beens who fled to Haiti after the war and who were only too happy to return to service. These active-duty assassins meet in these rooms, especially at night, to do the dirty work: beatings and interrogations, savage mutilations. The cries and groans of the tortured can be heard as far as the confines of Morne l'Hôpital and beyond.*

The assassination of these three young people is a new attempt at intimidation, intended to silence a generation that is beginning to make itself heard through student strikes and other actions. The government intends to gag anyone who speaks out against these crimes, but they must understand that we will never condone arbitrary and meaningless accusations and repression. As for the people, they must tell themselves that it is high time to turn the tide, and strike fear in the hearts of those who are terrorizing us.

I'm done the piece, but I can't for the life of me come up with a headline. And right away I begin to worry about the response.

That night is much the same as all the nights that have come before, these last few months. Darkness comes with its procession of mysteries and threatening shadows. Dogs bark in the distance, breaking the silence. Only they refuse to be muzzled; they know by instinct that they have to bite to fend off their attacker. Any chance of sleep is lost in a whirlwind of impatience and consternation at the complicit silence strangling the country. I know these executioners have been whetting their knives for a long time. I was in their sights even before they landed at the palace: in the early days, when we were fighting for women in this country to exercise their legitimate right to vote, I was already on their list. It's ironic that we were about to cross such a significant threshold, that women would have been able to vote for the first time, and instead ended up with a rigged election that brought this filth to power. The offensive against me was definitely launched because of what I've written, because I reminded people of these sham elections and because of my fervent condemnation of those who encourage the population to bury their heads in the sand. My editor made it clear: "Don't be surprised if you feel like you've been shunned."

I am aware of how exposed I am, and the loneliness weighs heavy on me. But I'll take this over surrender. My ship may be hit—badly, perhaps, it will roll and pitch, but the storm will eventually pass.

◆

A ravine runs on one side of the narrow path to my house, and there's no hedge or railing. Only now does it occur to me to be worried. I've lived in this house for years, and never before has the path seemed at all perilous, even in the rainy season. Now everything has changed. Danger lurks everywhere. We have all become potential liabilities—for our neighbours, for the state, for ourselves. We spy on each other, we are spied on, we ignore each other. Neighbours we thought were like family or who at least had become friends now turn away when we approach. Was it chance that the Deprez family, who were our neighbours for nearly twenty years, left their house last month without even saying goodbye? It makes me uneasy every time I think about it. Pedro Deprez, who could never keep away from the flutter of a skirt and who I had to turn down so many times, leaving like that, a moonlight flit? It's unfathomable. I can still hear his syrupy voice, feel his breath on my neck. One afternoon, I was sitting at the terrace at the Trois Marie sipping a beer, and he came up behind me without making a sound. I could sense someone staring at me intently, but I didn't want to turn around. He thought he was irresistible, with his youthful step and his cinnamon skin, that silky moustache, shiny black hair. He stepped forward and leaned over against the back of my chair. I shuddered. His wife was away on a trip, he told me, and did I want to come to Amany-les-Bains for the weekend. He placed his palm against my arm. His hand was too warm. I put down my glass, crossed my arms and just looked at him. Finally, he lowered his eyes, awkwardly tugged his panama hat back on, and left without another word. The smell of his cologne stayed with me until the evening. I imagine that a stud like him was seldom rejected, and sure enough, a few weeks later, he tried again. He must have thought I wasn't completely insensitive to his charms. He's obviously left the country, like so many others.

Carefully, I crouch down so that I can't be seen from the outside. My fingers resting on the windowsill, I peer into the night as if I want to steal its secrets. From time to time a light wind unravels a few clouds that darken the sky and hide the moon. I admire the silvery disc up there, sliding languidly in a knot of clouds. The moon is watery tonight, and we too are awash—in uncertainty, and in the crimes propped up by our silence and our treachery. We sink a little further each day.

The house is full of shadows and faceless voices, so many monsters prowling around. Even the silence has become awful, disturbing. Silence is the greatest peril, the enemy of this country. The night amplifies every noise: now I hear the plaintive bleating of a child, probably doubled over with hunger, unable to sleep. Still I scan the darkness, in vain. Nothing but silence. I listen, watchful, gasping at the slightest breath of wind. Am I going to end up afraid of my own shadow?

I think about my children. Soledad, the oldest, and the wildest, is studying abroad, in Spain. Since all this has been going on, I've been thankful she left, though that wasn't always the case.

"How well do you think you'll do in a country led by a man named Francisco Paulino Hermenegildo Teódulo Franco Bahamonde?" I asked her last year, half in jest, half horrified.

"He could just as well be called Baby Jesus," she snapped back, "it wouldn't have made any difference. I love Spain for what it is, I love the sky, and that's where I want to live."

"But Soli, the country is under the control of a dictator, how can you forget that?"

"In Nicaragua, Tacho Somoza," she began, "who assassinated Cesar Augusto Sandino with Washington's blessing, has been in power since 1936. Getulio Vargas established what he ironically calls the new state in Brazil, but which is actually an abominable dictatorship."

She went on, citing Argentina, then Paraguay, ground down by Stroessner. I had no idea, though she was showing me the open door; we were about to experience one of the most murderous dictatorships in America.

Soledad exudes a quiet strength that seems reckless, a calculated boldness that never ceases to dazzle and surprise me. She lives in Spain, she says, because the universe decided she should.

Félix and the girls have been staying in town at my sister Clarisse's house. It's much easier for them to go to school, though they don't really know how to deal with Clarisse's episodes, which are admittedly a cause for some concern. It makes me furious to consider how long I might have to be locked up.

In the dead of night, there's a thud outside. I shrink down, shaking. I can't hear anything else. Surely it's just a fruit that fell in the courtyard, a big papaya, maybe. Yet I am frozen, dazed. I can't think of anything else, nothing else exists in this precise moment but the insurmountable fear in my belly, a monstrous thing that nibbles at my nerves and curdles my blood. I slide along the wall against the cabinet without a sound, trying to find a slightly more comfortable position. The clock ticks and I count the minutes going by. I'm settling in for another night here, cowering behind the furniture like an animal being stalked. There's nothing I can do but wait for those who will come, sooner or later, today or tomorrow, I know it, to hold me to account.

HATRED IN HIS VEINS

MORE THAN EVER, these nights of terror force me to grapple with my solitude. I can't count on support or grace from anyone, I know that. Travellers lost in the desert must experience silence like this—an absence, a weight, a hole in the world. It's devastating, like dying too slowly. I've been told my pen is too sharp, that my refusal to comply—the rebel demon I insist on riding—will be the end of me. These warnings are barely veiled threats, many of them from Julio. Julio Séraphin is a cousin, a man for whom I had a great deal of respect for a long time. Maybe I appreciated his manners—he was always so affable—and those long-winded monologues of his. He can be mawkish, Julio, but he gets his own way somehow. Like many others, I was fooled. I understood too late that it was a clever way for him to spread his reactionary ideas.

I can't get him out of my mind; it's strange. He's usually so insistent, so why haven't I heard from him in almost a month? Bit by bit, a kind of panic comes over me, enfolding me, as if I were suddenly receiving a savage message from some mysterious source. Is it the feeling of coming upon a mystery? Julio! An avalanche of images—a voice, parts of a conversation I realize now I underestimated the importance of—come back to me. It was a Friday evening, Charles-Émile's birthday. We had just sat down to dinner. There were only six of us—Julio, who ate with us every Friday night, and Félix and the twins. Already people were beginning to stay home in the evenings. The children were in the living room playing a game of Monopoly, and Julio, Charlot, and I were in the kitchen. All of a sudden, Julio jumped up, looking flustered. An urgent phone call, he said. His usual smile looked forced. He was gone only briefly, but when he came back he looked out of sorts.

As usual, Charlot that night was boasting and blustering, blissfully listening to himself speak after having downed almost half a litre of whisky. When Julio came back to the table, the evening resumed, but the mood had turned murky. Julio was preoccupied and acted interested though he was clearly trying to conceal his bad mood.

"Trouble, cousin?" I asked. He brushed my question aside, waving his hand roughly. I was embarrassed by the rude gesture. I remember I got up to clear the table, and I picked up Charlot's empty glass, hoping to slow his bottomless thirst. Julio was watching me.

"People worry less, cousin," he told me, "when the table is set every day, when their plates are full and their glasses overflow with all the elixirs life has to offer. Worrying is for those whose stockings and soles are full of holes, those who can't afford to study. Those who don't even need pockets because they have nothing to put in them." He sneered. "I guess tossing out a few meaningless slogans on paper, or criticizing everything left and right isn't enough to change things."

I listened without interrupting until he was done, but I couldn't think of anything to say. I almost considered making an appointment with him to discuss his financial situation, but thought better of it. I didn't want to offend.

There was a moment of palpably awkward silence, then Charles-Émile, the eternal philosopher, spoke up, brashly, drunkenly breaking the silence.

"Dear, dear Julio," Charlot hiccupped, "we believe we are the masters of our own lives, we call ourselves masters, but we have no control over our own existence!"

Charles-Émile pounded the table, as if to give his words more heft. The dishes tinkled, the amber liquid sloshed in the glasses, and in the night the crickets' chirping had stopped. Julio's voice suddenly took up all the space.

"You don't know the half of it," he mocked, barely concealing his irritation. "If the moneyed likes of you have no control over their existence, imagine what it's like for those who get up every day and wait for bread that never comes."

How many times had Soledad tried to warn us about Julio? She was young and smart, smarter than all of us. "Hate runs in his veins," she said every time she saw him. "He reeks of hate like a drunkard reeks of alcohol." That evening, while Julio was talking, I watched him: his teeth were clenched, and he squeezed his fists open and closed. Charlot, who was no longer paying attention to Julio, went to the cupboard in search of another drink. I was stunned to see Julio glare at Charlot with such naked hatred. He tried to stay calm but his tone was razor-sharp. When Charlot returned with a glass full of whisky, ice cubes tinkling, Julio laid into him again.

"If I were you, cousin, I'd be looking for the address of a barber, get myself sheared. What are you trying to hide behind that bush of yours? It looks like it's eating your face. Do you know, there are rumours that from now on, they won't be satisfied with just rounding up tramps and vagrants. Anyone who's at all out of line will get chucked in one of those vans by men with dark glasses. They're going to rid the country of every man with a beard! And I certainly wouldn't want anything bad to happen to you. They're not going to ship you to the Sierra Maestra! Watch out, cousin. What do you think, that the shrubbery on your face makes you look hard and manly? Toughness and virility are ornaments from within, my friend. Listen—" Julio lowered his voice and leaned in conspiratorially—"I'll tell you my opinion. The United States is so afraid of revolutionary contagion in this part of the Caribbean that they'll never let Cuba go. And France too, they won't let go of Guadeloupe, Martinique, French Guiana, not for anything. They'd rather have the devil himself in power in this country rather than see Haiti fall like Cuba did. We've got to be realistic."

I was completely taken aback, that evening, listening to Julio speak. The vehemence of his words chilled me. He threw Charlot one last disdainful look, full of all the ire in the world, the frustration of an unstable petit bourgeois.

After Julio left, I tried to go over the scene with Charlot, but all he wanted to do was go to bed and sleep off the drink. I was wide awake, my head filled with Julio's threats, his voice a strident whistle, and when at last I slept I dreamed of snakes and monsters. I tried to talk to Charlot again the next day, but it was useless.

"What do you think: have we been feeding a traitor? Is there a viper in our bosom?"

"You're being paranoid again," Charlot scoffed. "Julio is just bitter, like so many people in this country. Misery can turn even the most tender heart."

I raised my voice.

"Jealous, frustrated people are a threat, Charles-Émile!" I was almost screaming. "Can't you understand that? Have you forgotten that Julio still has a set of keys to our house? I'm warning you…"

"So what? He lived here for months. What are you warning me about?"

"We should never have let him keep the keys."

I remember how worried I was, and Charlot dismissed my concerns, as usual.

"Julio is just an idiot pretending to be an intellectual," Charlot laughed. "Why are you so afraid of him all of a sudden?"

I watched him stuff a whole banana into his mouth. Every meal was another chance to wonder what could possibly have attracted me to this man.

"Besides," he went on, rattling his spoon and staining the tablecloth, "why me? Why should I have to ask him for the keys back? He's your cousin, isn't he?"

Looking back now, it's all so clear: I was taken aback and caught in a dilemma. What was I supposed to do? The situation was no longer a matter of suspicion or intuition, but a real threat, though I couldn't quite put my finger on it, and it was weighing heavily on us.

Charles-Émile fell silent. He had moved his cup aside to spread his newspaper on the table. I knew that he was pretending to be absorbed in the news, hoping to ride out the storm. He flipped through that fish wrapper of a state newspaper without much enthusiasm—though, in spite of himself, and although he was only half paying attention, his disbelief at what he was reading was written all over his face. After a while, he folded the paper and tossed it on the sofa.

◆

The memories are disturbing. The threats are growing more distinct even as my strength drains from me like sediment washed away—in my arms, in my chest, in my belly, a current pulls inevitably toward despair.

Some time earlier, Julio had announced that he was starting an accounting firm. I congratulated him, warmly: Julio had been unsettled and aimless for so long. What I didn't know was that he had found his calling when he discovered that his interests—the interests of his pocketbook—were in line with those of the public administration, the government in power and their butchers. He landed a lucrative contract to handle military accounting.

I'm on the verge of tears…Just imagine the pretenses we have to concoct when we make a conscious decision to be that blind. What kind of a deal did Julio have to strike? He'd always been known for his fierce aversion to work of any kind. His main goal in life, as Clarisse used to say, was to avoid any work or effort, especially manual labour.

One night, I couldn't sleep and grabbed a book by Curzio Malaparte. Was it *Don Camaleo* or *The Skin*, I don't remember. I opened it at random, and the sentence I read shot through me like a bolt of lightning. This was right after the Bel-Air massacre, and people all over the country were talking about how savage the recruits were, all this new Duvalierist rot, the death squads going after anyone and everyone for any reason at all, laying the foundation for the edifice of terror to be built over the corpses of the working class. The chapter was about a man they said was showing off how zealous the new converts were, so much so that they didn't even spare their mothers and fathers. Is that what happened to Julio?

And to what extent have I knowingly overlooked what's been more obvious than ever since the arrival of the makout? Julio, so craven, so weak—he was the perfect soil to grow the seed that feeds the beasts.

My eyes are being pried open, and it hurts so much. Julio was everyone's eternal right-hand man. He's always looking for a leg up, he spends his life trying to get into everyone's good graces. He wakes up in the morning and he can slip into the cast-off robes of a staunch Marxist, rifle through his drawers for his intellectual pretensions, which give him licence to talk for hours as obscurely as possible about capital, labour power, rising social tensions, and inevitable salutary revolutions, and get lost in the wild meanderings of an iron-clad Malthusian discourse, only to bed down in a brown shirt. I am astounded by some people's lack of discernment, the nonchalance. And of course my own blind spot: how could I have been so naive?

I struggle to my feet. I am carrying the city, the weight of disappointment on my shoulders, my back. I drag myself to the table in the middle of the room, where there is a jug of water. I take the jug, and I am irritated to notice that my hands are shaking. I pour myself a glass and then return to my post in the corner by the cupboard. We have to break the cycle.

Sleep has forsaken me. The first two nights I lay on the floor, staring blankly off into the darkness. I managed to doze for only a few short minutes. When I don't see the cars on duty up on the hill, at night I stand at the window watching for ghosts in the dark. I am now a target to be shot down, a woman to shun. In these times of rumours and grisly expeditions, who is mad enough to venture into such a battle?

It's hot. On the floor, the coolness of the mosaic tile soothes me like a secret caress, a friendly touch. It makes me feel good. I remember when Charles-Émile left. In the days following his desertion, I learned that routine can be a formidable enemy. I can't deny the heartache of the first few days, looking at the bare closet, the empty space in that big bed. For a long time we'd only been together out of habit. Even our bodies came together without any joy at all. I sometimes wonder if Charles-Émile was just waiting for an opportunity to cut the cord that was strangling us both. He decided he had to give me a full, detailed explanation, a realistic picture of the situation. Faced with the rampage that awaits us, he told me, my word weighed less than a hummingbird feather. "They'll break you," he repeated, frightened. It was like listening to a complete stranger. Did he believe he could convince me with arguments like that? It was hard for me to accept that the man who said he loved me and whom I had loved was saying this, foretelling my death. Had I made a mistake or was it Charles-Émile who didn't know me? One of Clarisse's favourite theories was that we were strangers to ourselves. "How can we pretend to know someone well?" she would ask. "That's quite a claim, isn't it, Mika? The man might snore next to you every night but he's still a stranger to you." Maybe she's right, maybe I'm always wrong: wrong fight, wrong mark, wrong man.

One night, when I was wracked with fear—people everywhere were commenting on an article of mine, "The Sacrifices of Bel-Air," saying it was inflammatory, but really I had only demanded justice against the perpetrators of one of the most monstrous massacres in our history, another massacre—that night, Charlot was berating me, the worst accusations, and he told me I should leave with the children. "A lot of people are leaving," he warbled. Again, I refused. He had run out of arguments. I was putting our family at risk, he told me.

"You're taking unnecessary risks. Don't you know that in some societies journalism is considered a pastime for idle women?"

It was sick, it was an obsession, he added, "a refuge for those who feel aggrieved by great literature." He knew how to hit me where it hurt. He ground his teeth, and his words drilled at my temples.

"I'm telling you, Mika, we haven't seen anything yet. This is only the beginning, the tip of the iceberg. Let me say it again: the United States is openly supportive, and they'll never accept another revolution in the Caribbean. You know as well as I do that the Americans would rather blow up the island and bury us all. Don't say I didn't warn you."

I chose to stay silent. Had Charles-Émile also joined the ranks of those who learn to carefully disguise their tails and talons, to drop their spines lower than they were even asked? He just crept along, he didn't trust his own shadow, his voice.

I shouldn't dwell on their words, Julio and Charles-Émile—the man I'm already calling my late husband. But it's no use. I try to think of lighter things, but my belly tightens. Can I loosen the knot, which is getting tighter as the hours go by? It seems impossible. I would have to scratch out all those deaths, bury them in the depths of my soul, cross out the faces of the three young men who were just slaughtered by cowards. Three young people with bright futures. They were as old as my own children. The pain has no name, it's voracious. My article is there, on the desk. I read it, I reread it so many times. Nothing can stop me from speaking out, nothing will shut me up.

AS NIGHT FALLS

CHARLES-ÉMILE PACKED HIS BAGS when the anonymous midnight calls started getting more insistent and more threatening. I had published two articles in the weekly *L'Aube*, "Who shall be silenced?" and "When shall we drink from this overflowing cup?" In the first piece, I stressed the importance of freedom of speech—for men, women, and children. For all citizens.

Is it any wonder that such a small country has such high illiteracy rates? The reason is quite simple: those who have always had a monopoly on power, and therefore on what is said, have no interest in ensuring that everyone learns to read and write. But they don't squander a single opportunity to brag, shouting from the rooftops that we live in a free country. It is a shameless lie.

In countries that claim to be free, countries where citizens are truly free, the fundamental freedom each person has is nothing less than the fruit of freedom of speech. In free countries, men and women are free without condition, and women have the right to speak by any means available—first and foremost the press and the newspapers. The acquired right to freedom of speech, this right women have won, is invaluable, and all credit is due to them. Year after year, century after century, despite the repression they suffer, if women had been content to remain locked in the smothering fold of family and friends, where they would have mouldered, if they had been forever content with the limits set for them by those who claim to guide them, they would never have known any other life than enslavement.

Can a society that bullies and shackles its people, which feels nothing but contempt for them, claim to be free? We are at a time when women's struggle for freedom of speech has nothing to do with cheap feminism, based as it is solely on the values advocated by a caste of the blessed, by a handful of the well-to-do. We do not dream of utopia, we simply dream of speaking freely, to allow us to build a true society of free women and men. Free speech alone shall guide us toward the dialogue that is essential to accessing a more just and therefore a freer world. We do not seek free speech in order to sit among our sisters in petticoats beneath the arbour. We do not seek free speech as a facade. We shall speak out of duty and in the name of freedom to fight prejudice and to banish ignorance, that ignorance so carefully upheld on our island, the ball and chain that prevents us from moving forward. From now on, we shall occupy every space where speech may flourish, to be able to say a clear, resounding No! to all injustice in the name of all the voiceless women and men of this country.

The newspaper *L'Œdipe* called it "a declaration of war on the Supreme Leader and therefore on the nation." Two days after the article came out, I found the envelope with my death warrant slipped under the fence.

◆

Did I sleep? I have the horrible sense of having been unconscious, which feels nothing like the restfulness that sleep provides. My left arm is numb and I have a dull ache in my lower back. The curtains are drawn and the studio is dark. I don't turn on the lamp just yet. I'm afraid of the night, but I'm also afraid of the day, I'm afraid even of the slap of my footsteps on the tiles. I fumble to the toilet, my feet finding their way. When I come back, I lift a corner of the heavy curtain, carefully. It's already daylight, though the morning is grisly and grey. On a shelf in the library there is a photo of Charles-Émile and me. I take the frame in my hand and sink into his favourite armchair. I stare at the photograph, asking silent questions. Soledad took it, so long ago, one day when we were both reading in our bedroom. The window is open behind us and a breeze fills the curtains. Charles-Émile has an expression on his face that might be interpreted as tenderness. The snapshot is years old. As Clarisse would say, everything in life has an expiry date, don't you know. Enough of this wordless conversation; I curl up in bed. A few minutes of rest will do me good. After a night on the hard floor, the softness of the sheets is a comfort, as always.

On my bedside table, there's a copy of *Don Quixote*, a gift from Charles-Émile. He took great pains with the inscription, writing half a page. He thought it pertinent to define Bovarysm, to specify, *there is, in this magnificent work, the world as it is and the world as Don Quixote wanted to see it*. I usually open *Don Quixote* at random—any given page offers up all the comedy in the world, spinning free as the blades of a windmill. I appreciate the onslaught against religion, the straight-shooting, prosaic Sancho. Seething, I rip out the page where Charles-Émile waxes poetic—a real gem, or so he thought—insipidly mixing *old rose, cardboard armour, orphans to rescue, and kingdoms to protect...*

◆

Today is the fifteenth of September. There's a vernissage tonight organized by a group of painters, including Clarisse. I have to make an appearance, after filing my article. I'll have to sleep at Bé and Jeanne's, or at Clarisse's place. I don't know if I can handle Clarisse and her moods the night after an opening. Do I have the strength? I decide to stay at Bé's.

I would gladly do without this outing, but Clarisse would hate me. She's been so busy putting together the exhibit that I haven't seen her for weeks. Tante Jeanne begged her not to participate. "This is not the time," she pleaded, trembling. "This country has never seen a bloodier election." All the more reason, according to Clarisse, to go on with our lives, with work, to say no to the persecution and the silence thrust upon us. Has Jeanne forgotten what we're made of? "Her mind is starting to go," Clarisse says. "Everything that lives softens with age." The last time we saw each other, when we had lunch at Bé's one Sunday, Clarisse was furious. "Cancel?" she screamed at Jeanne. "You might as well tell me to go hang myself!"

◆

I'm incredibly emotional as I leave the house to go to the newspaper office to drop off my article. I walk around the house three times, making sure all the doors are closed, the shutters locked. Should I take the car or should I walk? I could take shortcuts to try to shake the men who are tailing me. The idea that they would catch me and tip my car over into the ravine has been nagging at me since morning. In the end, I slip on my flats. I will walk through the narrow lanes and alleyways that wind down to the bottom of the hill to get to the church square, and from there I'll get a taxi.

In the garden, I look for what caused the thud I heard in the night, which gave me such a fright. It turns out it was neither a papaya nor a soursop, and in any event, they're not in season. An object right beneath my bedroom window stops me dead in my tracks. There, under the bougainvillea, lies a large rock, one of those enormous stones polished by the sea. It must weigh at least four kilos. How could anyone have thrown it so far? I stand there for a long time, rattled, staring at the object. Two crosses are painted on the rock, in blood and tar.

On the road, I'm a robot, my knees are about to give way. I pull myself up stiffly, I fight against fear, I fight against my limbs, which somehow are no longer quite attached to my body. I fight against this body which itself is no longer flesh, not muscle and bone. I am no more than a bundle of raffia carried by the wind off the mountain. If they dared throw that rock right under my window, what will they do next?

When I finally get to the office, it's hard to tell what my colleagues are thinking. They're skittish, like prey. They all look constipated. Several are too busy to talk to me, flustered by the harshness of the daily routine, their personal lives, all their worries and concerns. It's a heavy burden. There's Jacques Lafontaine, whose wife left him. He hugs me without a word, but his body speaks for him—he's a broomstick, floating in his rumpled suit. They say his wife, Andrée Claude, ran off with a makout, a man named Justin Bertrand, a real skunk, a rainmaker in Babiole. When Papa Dòk came to power he was appointed Minister of Health and got as rich as Croesus. Jacques is getting death threats, and suffering in silence: he can't ask for divorce or see his children. One afternoon last month, he dropped me off at home and we had coffee. He told me a bit about what was going on. He blamed himself for not having been able to hang on to Andrée Claude. "What can we do," I replied, "against their talons? The problem isn't so much whether you'd have been able to keep her or not; those scavengers leave us the scraps they choose." When I came back from the kitchen with the tray and the cups, I saw he'd laid out his treasures—photos of his children and his wife.

Salnave gets up from his desk to come hug me, to welcome me. I'd rather not think about what this act of courage will cost him; even here I've made enemies. Some people believe I'm jeopardizing the newspaper, that I should be more moderate now. Salnave asks for news from the street; he's about to head home.

"Brace yourself. It's no picnic. It took me almost two hours to get here!"

He looks surprised.

"You know, it's not that it's especially long. It's just hard to get around. The streets are packed with people, everyone's disoriented. There are crowds everywhere, people dashing out to get supplies as if they were afraid of a siege or a hurricane. And the military has invaded the square in the front of Saint-Charles. When I got there to take a taxi, there were four tarped army trucks in the square."

Salnave is livid.

"This is a provocation!" he cries. "They're trying to scare the students, keep them locked up at home night and day. They know they meet there, in the square."

"Most of the women who run stands under the flamboyants weren't there when I went by. They've fled the killings too, and the soldiers who robbed them or refused to pay."

"It was the same craziness this morning at rush hour. People were panicking, everyone was afraid, looking up at the houses the night marked with tar and blood."

I lower my voice and tell him about the stone I found under my window, the cars on duty at night, at the bottom of the hill.

Salnave goes pale.

"You have to watch out, Mika!" His voice catches. "They're tightening the noose, and they'll stop at nothing, you know that. Did you listen to the radio this morning?"

"No, I can't take it anymore. I don't want to listen to him! Any more and I'm going to throw the radio in the garbage."

"Well, just imagine, all the stations have been ordered to read a chapter of Duvalier's catechism every day on the airwaves."

"Bastards! Fear gnaws at our bellies, and they're celebrating."

"Truer words, Mika. Never in their entire existence have these—these…subhumans experienced such joy. Apparently, two of them, two of Chambelland's men, who'd just been recruited and appointed commanders of the Volunteers in their district, dropped dead, apparently struck down for having tested the extent of their powers, the boundless authority that sanctions the worst madness. It turns out that being aware of your own dominance, which these men abuse shamelessly, is a deadly drug."

"May they all die of intoxication, drunk on the knowledge that they are so feared. And as quickly as possible, so we can be rid of them."

"We're not going to be able to get rid of these bastards so quickly, Mika. The propaganda machine is running full tilt. Devilish power like this is fed by fierce ideologues, we mustn't forget that, and they're propping up the regime. You wouldn't believe the feathers this son of Lucifer has been able to tuck in his cap, without even really having to ask. His cabal is full of men who for some obscure reason want to earn their halo, that prestige—among them the two Blanchet men, another one, Berrouet, and Boyer, Bayard, Désinor, the goon Pomereau, and of course the infamous Mercier, the man of a thousand faces. And Jean Magloire, you must have heard of him; he runs *L'Œdipe*. He's at the head of that team, who claim that their hands are clean."

"Tell me, Salnave, is it true that those men helped create his… catechism?"

"Are you surprised?"

"My sister Clarisse told me otherwise, that it was the work of an insignificant little group that calls itself the Sovereign."

"The ones who bark away on the radio, singing Duvalier's praises? You mean St-Lot, Dominique, Laferrière, that riffraff? Actually, they're more like enforcers, maybe. Secondary propagandists? I've heard they're recruiting students, luring them into fake revolutionary ambushes and then throwing them to the dogs. These marauders have some skills; long before Duvalier came to power, they helped put together Duvalier's *Essential Works*. What a peculiar, mediocre book."

Salnave and I chat, and around us the typewriters clatter as loudly as ever, drowning out our voices. The secretary tells me that a meeting scheduled for the following Monday has been postponed indefinitely. That the article I just filed, which I worked so hard on, will be published at some point in the future. I take it in, unflinching. The newspaper is on shaky ground, like everything else.

A swarm of insignificant, anxious bourgeois crowd the doors of the hall at Bas Peu de Chose: pursed lips, bowties, women in formal dress, stiletto heels and red nails, forced laughter. It goes either way, here; dread makes people either laugh or tremble. As soon as I get there, I want to run away. For a moment I think I might faint, and I begin to run out of air as Clarisse takes the stage on behalf of the artists' group. But she's spent and in the end says very little. Those who get it read between the lines, enthralled by one of her paintings—the largest, entitled *Quand descend la nuit*—as night falls, a reference to Apollinaire, who foresaw totalitarianism looming in Europe: *Let night fall on our foreboding, unbroken path of blood.* Clarisse's paintings are becoming more and more abstract; every day her lines, her curves and colours are increasingly uninhibited, bound only by her mood.

I don't stay long. I'm being watched, tracked. I can't stop seeing the stone under my window. As I leave, I snap a picture of a poster on the front of the building: *Ten Voices for a New Beginning*, it reads. The whole group made it; it's a huge canvas. There's something oppressive about it, a ruthlessness redolent of the German expressionists.

RAW OCTOBER

It's almost October. Between the war songs and the propaganda speeches, press releases about the celebrations for Duvalier's swearing-in are taking up all the airwaves and every inch of the daily papers.

October is a sacred month, when school starts again after the summer holidays, but this time it wears a different face. All the schools have been commandeered to house Duvalier's troops. Swaggering across the countryside, the butchers organized raids, forcing who knows how many peasants—whom they openly despise—to leave their land. They shipped them to the capital to boost the crowds gathered there to applaud the autocrat. They flocked from the provinces and communes and poured into the cities, crammed into huge trucks normally used for transporting livestock. Once the schools are full, these poor people are dumped out in the streets, parked on the sidewalks. Port-au-Prince is now home to the largest slave market in the Caribbean. We see them marching in endless parades, dressed in their thick blue shell coats with guns slung across their shoulders. Many of them, to their great misfortune, are wearing shoes for the first time, and they limp along like broken men, their feet enclosed in too-big used army boots recovered by the government from who knows where. What a distressing spectacle, this noisy tide, panting under the sun. We see them marching by, sweating like farm animals, coming to cheer for a despot who doesn't even care to feed them. Far from their plots and their daily lives, they steal, snatch, and extort what they can so they don't starve to death.

While the schools are occupied by troops, education—a symbol of hope—is trampled by the powers that be. Students are seen as potential enemies. All you have to do now is put on a blue canvas uniform and a red scarf, hoist a rifle and pistols, and you become a militiaman, a leader, almighty. The horizon is getting darker by the day, Duvalierist vermin swarming on all sides.

It's Sunday, October 20. Two more days before the charade hits its apex. The walls, fences, posts, and awnings are plastered with posters and banners with threatening slogans: *I AM the revolution. Whoever goes against it stands against ME! Duvalierism is the only way to bring the country out of misery. Opponents shall be charged with treason!*

This morning, Charlot's voice on the telephone. It's funny, I had almost forgotten what he sounds like, the timbre of his voice. Time heals, it's true. How distant those days seem now, when simply his voice was enough to light a fire in me. For an instant, I forget that he's there, my thoughts wandering. I wonder how we choose our partners. Why was it I fell into this man's arms? Is love as blind as we say it is? All my life with Charlot, I wondered about my need for him, until my body itself grew tired of his shortcomings. Clarisse, of course, never missed an opportunity to tease me. "If I were you, I would get rid of that body of yours," she told me. "It betrays you, it doesn't know how to choose."

Charlot's voice seems as detached as my desire for him. Has he known since those scoundrels seized power that he would end up floating downstream, to cooler waters?

Have his daughters come home, he wants to know. Are they planning to stay in the city? Do I know how to reach them? He seems unusually concerned about the children, and I wonder why. He was in town this morning, didn't he see the signs and banners everyone is talking about? The students have put up barricades all around the Faculty of Ethnology, there are tanks plowing around on the main streets. Is it true? Charles-Émile is evasive. He only saw what everyone is talking about.

With these last elections, we have moved toward the knife-edge, we are about to tip over into the void, and Charlot still has no idea, no real opinion. All he wants is to keep filling his bowl. His architecture firm is doing well. A new clique is getting richer, buildings are going up, business is booming. The old guard has eaten enough and now we're setting the table for a new feast.

The familiar impatience in his voice brings me back to the conversation.

"No," I reply, "the girls haven't come home. I'll ask them to call you. Yes, I'll be sure to remind them to be careful."

"We have to learn to read the signs," he says, a little too quickly.

And I understand that he says these words without really thinking, just to have something to say, anything. But he should have kept his mouth shut, because now I'm hounding him again.

"What do you mean by that? What's going on? What are you planning?"

He has nothing to say to any of my questions.

"It's been an off day," he finally says blandly.

I answer very slowly. "October is expiring in fear and shame. Our schools have been taken over by lackeys. At the rate this is going, who knows when the children will be able to set foot there again?"

He doesn't answer. Bé is coming over, I tell him. Useless words, like his, spoken to fill the silence.

"She's fed up with the city. The noise, the sirens, the steady stream of vicious brutes armed to the teeth. It's making her sick. She'd rather see me here."

Now Charlot stops dodging. He's aggressive, his words a knife.

"You're even crazier than they say!" he bleats. "Don't you ever think a little? You know Bé has no respect for anything! She lies, she's never been able to hold her tongue. Do you think she's going to start now? It's unsafe, and you're more exposed than ever, Mika." He tries to lower his voice, to soften his words.

I'm stunned. I shut up, but Charlot goes on, hammering at me.

"Don't they have enough against you already? Against your whole family, for that matter. You probably haven't given it a second thought. Why don't you have Clarisse over too, while you're at it? The emancipated artist...Doesn't she know that there's a long list of people who have scores to settle with her? They could round you all up at the same time! You'd make it easy."

It's a good thing he's not in front of me, since I would have given him the licking of his life. I start screaming—the whole neighbourhood must be able to hear me, but I don't care.

"A thousand times I curse the womb that you sprang from, you son of a hyena, mongrel dog that you are. We are where we are today because of cowards like you."

"Are you listening to me, Mika?" he says. But I'm unhinged, I can't hear anything.

"Do you know how lucky you are right now, you scum seed, you inglorious wretch? Of course you don't know, it's absurd. And thank God. Because you will never be able to imagine how I would have delighted in ripping out your shitty little mouth with my fingernails."

I hang up.

I've long since closed the book on Charles-Émile, on us; there is nothing left but dust. In thick layers, it spreads everywhere, choking me, and Charlot's fingerprints are slow to fade. So many images pop up out of nowhere, a relentless rush of reminders. It's infuriating. But why today, why the welter of memories precisely when everything around me is falling apart? The more I try to banish these memories, the more another part of me persists in summoning them. They invade me. I am like someone condemned who, seeing that the end is nigh, goes on a spree, to clean, to purge. Perhaps I'm saying goodbye. I think back to how much shit I've swallowed, the years with Charlot, and it's all there, heavy and unmistakable. That's the weight of illusions and remorse, my sister would say, to describe what I used to call a complicated happiness.

I hate the thought of another reckoning, one too many. With disconcerting clarity, I am reliving those days when, after a week without hearing from him at all, he would just suddenly show up for lunch. *The pig returns to sniff the pen*, I thought to myself each time. After eating, we would take a nap while the children played in the garden under the watchful eye of Tante Bé. Charlot never asked how the children were doing, did they need him, what were they doing in school. Everything was owed him. He had become a father like any self-respecting man and it was perfectly normal for him to have a wife to take care of his offspring. His indifference to girls, especially, was appalling. So often, because they are girls, they're not given even as much thought as the furniture. It's regressive, but above all it's selfish, a chronic egoism that oozes up from the foundation of paternalistic societies. How often have I tried to talk about this with him? Not that he ever showed much interest. It was always too much to ask.

Sometimes we would make love, quickly. Very quickly, he would come, and that was it, he was content. It was disconcerting, but I didn't have time to think. Maybe I didn't want to think, grateful for the crumbs.

Like a blind beast, when he showed up like that, he threw himself on me, grunting as he plowed into me. How shameful that I made myself believe I put up with it just to have peace. He rushed into my body, jubilant and impatient. His animal ways baffled me. That's how I saw Charles-Émile. In those moments, his eagerness to possess me frightened me, because it was silent. Our relationship seemed to be only about sex, about the sexual organ—his. There was never a tender word, not even some banal sentiment. His absolute refusal to speak to me tenderly when I was giving myself to him, even when I didn't want to, was doubly hurtful: his brutality, and my own against myself. How heinous...But I persisted with the whole mortifying relationship, the horrible feeling that I was merely an object of his, like his shoes, his car keys, his money. What was the difference, I asked myself once, between the settlers long ago who stamped their livestock and had their way with any woman they liked, and my relationship with Charlot, like so many of the men around me and those who agree to be their partners? Often they struggled, like fiends in a holy font, against the crippling masculine heritage that imposed such abominable ways of treating their companions, and spewed rhetoric that was meant to be progressive but which they rarely managed to put into practice. It was a difficult dilemma, because I was fully aware of the battle between the two women within me: the one who wanted to keep her head above the muddy water and fight back, and the other, who bore the scars of a backwards, conformist society and who in order to make sense of it resorted to endless philosophical analysis, wading about in pretentious intellectual nonsense, speaking vaguely about teaching love, teaching tenderness. How can love be taught? Is it even possible to reach someone whose heart is on backwards and whose mind is addled?

How many years did I stay in the cesspool Clarisse called my purgatory? Did I accept my share of contradictions too complacently?

I shouldn't brood like this, I've already spent too much time going around in circles. I have to stop dwelling on it, even though I know the rancour will remain for a long time to come, like a stone in my mouth.

BRIGAND'S BALL IN THE BROTHEL OF THE LORD

BÉ HAS BEEN OVER AT THE HOUSE with me for a few days, as she wanted. She tries hard to be discreet, but from time to time she tiptoes hesitantly into the study like a beggar to offer me something—to freshen my water or get me some tea. Her presence is both a comfort and a concern. What happens if there is an attack, or if the house gets shot at?

Early November. Twilight, like a mantle of mourning, comes quickly. Then a dull silence as the night takes hold of everything. But today, dusk brings along some ruckus about the inauguration tomorrow. Toni runs over, despite the fear, to bring us the latest news. Has she lost her mind? She's so reckless. She cut through the middle of the thicket—she's afraid of being seen by the militia in case they're still out on the road—and charges in, drenched in sweat. Her words tumble out, confused. "When will this noise end?" she asks me. I confess I'm losing my mind too. Throughout the afternoon, all we could hear was the chaotic howl of people and animals, a metallic thrum, the blare of horns, vaksin, trumpets, and drums. The sky went dark, as if it were filled with anger. Toni tells us that down in town, they're going around with their rifles on their shoulders, knocking on doors to hand out crucifixes painted red and black. The makout have decreed that all Vodou priests, manbos, Catholic priests, and pastors must be at their service.

"What the devil have we fallen into?" I ask Bé. "Are we going to be able to hold out?"

"The situation is explosive, but it's got to stop. We will hold out, you can be sure of that," Bé says. "They'll have to stop!"

I nod, timidly. I'd love for her to be right.

"Hope alone isn't enough to dismantle the system, Bé."

My voice is a faint whisper, and suddenly I start to cry. I sniffle, tears rolling down my cheeks. Too late; all the emotions of the past few months have put my nerves to the test. I am spent.

"Are you forgetting, my girl, that even the MacDonald stopped?" A runaway train is one thing; this madness won't subside so easily.

Tante Bé hasn't seen me cry since I was a child. She's startled, and dejected: she knows I rarely cry. I feel guilty for blubbering around two old women. There's no way they can defend themselves against this madness. But I can't help it… "Do you realize that the three of us are alone in this big house, isolated here at such a dangerous time?"

Bé silences me with a gesture of her hand, calm but vigorous.

"We are not alone, Mika."

I wait for her to continue but she gets up and goes to the window. She sits sideways, and for a long time she contemplates the darkening road, from which a constant, threatening growl arises. She looks back at Toni and me. "Their trucks are moving in, trucks full of killers. They're going to invade the whole city at dawn. Yet we must not give in."

Bé's voice, firm and full of conviction, is a whip. I know that voice, her tone is so familiar, I've always known it. She will not tolerate a single thoughtless word. For a second I remember how she would stand up to my father or Clarisse. That voice; she never shouted or lost herself in needless antagonism. It's a voice that comes from the womb, with such quiet strength and assurance that whoever hears it is struck dumb.

Bé stares at me. "I'm surprised at you, my girl, at your words. That's not how I brought you and your sister up. Don't you dare say we're alone. We're not half-women! We look upon death—death, which has been lurking for nearly a whole year, but the deaths we mourn must compel us to hold our heads higher each day. Trials and privation, humiliation, kidnappings…None of it will make me a victim! Do you hear me, Mika? I have to grab fear by the collar, and you should do the same. Otherwise death wins."

Tante Bé has her own notion of existence: her tendency to refer to proverbs, to the past, but also to her own experience, all of it feeds her abiding conviction that human beings come into the world in order to fight. Her basic maxim is that you are only alive if you are ready to fight.

Bé reminds us yet again of the MacDonald train derailment. She doesn't recall exactly when it happened, but her retelling is vivid: the train tore through the town like a wild animal.

"It had gone for miles and miles. You'd have thought it would go on forever. There wasn't a building that could stop it, no pillars, bridges, or barriers. The MacDonald was loose. The damage was as bad as the most savage of hurricanes. But then there was the Pic Macaya. They collided like two rival beasts, and the mountain, without lifting a finger, sent the MacDonald flying into the Artibonite River, where its rusting remains still lie."

In a superhuman effort to tame my trepidation, or to show Bé that I am worthy of her, I offer to walk Toni home. I don't dare ask her to sleep over, that would just be too risky: every night, I count the hours, hoping for morning. Before she leaves, Toni reaches into her bra and pulls out a piece of paper folded umpteen times. She unfolds it carefully, smoothing it flat with her hands. She asks us to pray with her. Bé doesn't mind, mainly out of friendship for Toni.

Bé hates priests, pastors, houngans, and all the rest of them as much as Clarisse does. They have too much power, they say. Toni reassures her: the most powerful vibration in the universe, she explains, is prayer. She tells us to close our eyes and gather our thoughts. Toni's voice trembles with faith, frequently tested.

"Almighty God and all the saints in heaven, as we await the great day of deliverance, we ask that you grant us strength and support. Keep us, protect us; in you we place our trust. Saint Jude, patron of desperate causes, listen to us and help us out of this hardship. Saint

Anthony, you who know where all things are that have gone astray, bring us peace. Saint Augustine, who has the power to shun the rats and all the vermin and parasites, get rid of the Duvalierist dreck that is ruining this country and take away the terror that paralyzes us. Saint Louis, you who know abscesses so well, see that all these rabid dogs die quickly. Saint Barbara, let us be rid of all this carrion as soon as possible. Saint Benedict, they are all evildoers and swear only by evil spells; let them poison and destroy each other."

By the time Saint Fiacre comes around, whose help is implored to get rid of haemorrhoids, Bé reminds Toni that it will be dark soon. Maybe it would be best to continue the prayers on the way home.

Toni and I walk one behind the other because the path to her house is narrow and crowded with weeds. We tread slowly, weighed down by the horror that surrounds us on every side. It only takes about ten minutes, but it seems like forever. Toni quietly reels out an unbelievable litany that would have given Clarisse quite a laugh. I follow her, slowing my steps because she can't go very fast.

When I get back, Bé and I fall asleep huddled together, like in the old days, when I was a child. I used to wake in the dark and go slip into her arms. Barefoot, creeping down the long corridor where the bedrooms were lined up, I would work out my plan: *I'm going to tell her that I've felt nauseous for a few days.* I would stop and think. *Better to be careful, Bé has to believe me.* There I was, moving my lips, working out the flaw in my plans, searching in my little head filled with ghosts and steam-snorting horses with metal hooves, wondering what perils might stir Tante Bé's sympathy so she'd let me sleep in her bed. Now, with Bé here, I've left my hideaway against the big cabinet in the study. That night, I sleep a little bit longer. I dream of flying pigs, of women shucking their skins and soaring through the neighbourhood gobbling up newborns. When their escapade is over, the flying cannibal women are chased by the MacDonald train while militiamen with hippopotamus mouths jump from the moving train to gut them, their carnassial teeth as long as swords.

◆

An insistent chime draws us from our dreams. Frozen with dread, we wonder if it might be the fire brigade, but Bé reminds me that there are no firefighters in the city. It's true: we watch houses burn as if it were a show. When a house catches fire, well, it must be because its occupants deserve it, it can only be a punishment. If by chance there's a hydrant nearby, the punishment is mitigated, because you can count on the solidarity of the whole neighbourhood forming a human chain, buckets full of water passed down to appease the demons who've decided to engulf the house and its inhabitants. I rush to the window. The ungodly racket must mean the festivities have started up again, Bé points out.

"The brigands are back at it," Bé sighs. "But the second half has a much more elegant name: here comes the *Te Deum* now," she announces, pursing her lips comically.

We decide to follow the broadcast of this masquerade on the radio with Toni, who flits over again today. She's too nervous and especially too worried to stay alone, she says. According to the announcer, the butchers are meeting with all the churches of the country, with much fanfare. At the cathedral in Port-au-Prince, he purrs, a ceremony will be held to bring together dignitaries and distinguished embassy staff.

"Grim bacchanals," Bé laments. "The country's new masters are all there. What I wouldn't give to see all those priests and Monsignors—servants of the great Satan, fierce defenders of the regime…That must be quite the shoving match, all of them in their ceremonial robes elbowing each other out of the way; all that bowing and scraping."

"Quiet!" Toni shushes her. While Bé rants, the announcer is listing names: "The bishops Kebreau, Ligondé, Agénor, and other priests, like Father Georges and Father Papayer…"

"Their job is to recruit needy students—nothing too complex— and hand them over to the thugs," Bé goes on.

Toni sighs, annoyed. "I should have stayed home," she sulks.

I can't hear anything the announcer is saying.

"But you don't understand!" Bé bellows. "I can see them from here, these men's hands are stained by so much blood, puffing their chests out. They have no shame. It makes me want to scream. And tomorrow we'll have their faces on the front page of the newspaper, because they're the first to force their way to the front of the canopy. They have all the space they want now that they've run the uncooperative clergy into exile or thrown them in jail."

"The followers of the father of the nation," the announcer continues, "have formed a human barricade all around him. We can see the architects—Barbot, Tassy, Franck Romain, Ti Boulé, Gros Féfé, Ti Bobo, Saint-Albin, Abel, Jérôme, Kanbronne, Daumec, Gérard, Louis, Cinéas—the police prefect, Day, and so many others."

Bé angrily snaps the radio shut. "That macabre edifice won't be coming down any time soon."

Toni is clearly dismayed and terrified.

"So many people," Bé wipes away a tear, "must be watching these monsters strut around and sobbing as I am for not having been able to read the signs. You can't say it wasn't obvious, that's for sure."

I must look baffled. Bé stands up, upset.

"I'm talking about those who felt the thrill of the election campaign. I can still hear all of them, complicit, on the airwaves of all the radio stations, those tribunes of doom campaigning for Duvalier. Today we know that they were gravediggers, their tongues scooping out graves for so many people who were marked by the regime's vindictiveness. For a long time now we have been hostages of these monsters—they're not humans—with their simple speeches and their lethal language. Remember, Toni? Do you remember all those voices on the radio: *So-and-so, you have the floor!* That gruesome circus, their calculated indemnity...They paved the way for the makout. They took the floor and left the rest of us without a voice. And now, today, they are tossing the souls of our people on the pyre and reaping the rewards for their work. They must be elated, those courtesans, trussed up in their abominable red and black."

Bé comes out of the room, running almost, as if she's fleeing from some grim spectacle. She shuts herself in the kitchen and I can hear her scrabbling around, rummaging in the cupboards. She must be cleaning, or looking for a bite, to try to calm down. She's going to make herself sick, choking down food whole like that. Trying to eat her anger.

With Bé out of the room, I turn the radio back on and listen to the commentary. The announcer is obviously overwhelmed. From time to time, he stutters, stumbles over his words, lops off a syllable here and there. I hope to God his fumbling won't get him headed straight for the firing squad. I shudder: *and now, arriving at the cathedral*, the announcer says, *the First Lady*—that yellow-skinned woman who's always made up like a clown for public appearances.

The host's voice is muffled by the loud applause that greets her.

"It's probably that ghastly band of sabre-toothed females, led by Rosalie Bosquet and that madame Lalanne, who are clapping like that," Toni whispers.

"The applause is sinister, like the beating of crows' wings," I tell Toni. "Her name is Simone Ovid."

"I know," Toni replies. "And she must have those four puffy-faced runts shuffling their feet by her side. I saw them at the Champ de Mars during an army parade. Three girls—that day, they were dressed up in these red tulle dresses—and one boy, about eight years old, walking ahead. He looks like some kind of amphibian. And believe it or not, Mika, he was carrying a huge machine gun!"

A power outage puts an end to the misery, and Toni goes home. Disoriented, Bé and I take refuge in bed and spend the whole morning there.

Later, Toni tells us about a scene that everyone was talking about, but which apparently wasn't broadcast. The makout leader's wife, nicknamed Madame Zonbi because of her vacant look, went crazy all of a sudden, claws out, demanding that they give her the canopy.

Without a word, and bowing like a maniac, one of the bishops placed the umbralucum over her head. Little by little, two horns started to poke through, piercing the cloth. The president himself wore a cassock and his eternal bowler hat. He never takes it off, probably because it covers his own horns. With his zonbi consort on his arm, he opened the ceremony. As for his wife, she stuck two candles on the horns that had just sprouted.

◆

What a peculiar day. Nature itself is rebelling, like on the eve of a storm. In late afternoon, gusts of wind sweep through the city. People run around without knowing where to go, hiding under shaky porches on the verge of disintegrating, scrambling for space under tattered awnings. Is this a nightmare? The waking dream of uneasy minds? Sadly, no. Doors hanging half off their hinges slam with an awful bang, and sheets of steel and bits of rusty metal dance through the air, threatening to decapitate passers-by, before landing on the branches and shrubs that have fallen into the middle of the road. Petrified, the population barricades itself in a silence deeper than the tomb.

I come into the kitchen; something smells delicious. In front of the stove, Bé is humming. She's prepared a goat fricassee. "Let's eat before the world ends," she says bitterly.

"I'm sure if you call Toni and tell her what you're cooking, she'll come over," I suggest.

"I was thinking of phoning her, but I doubt she'll come back, even if the wind dies down. I know it won't last, even strong as it seems. But I know Toni. She must be in bed, trembling, convinced that the hurricane has been ordered by Satan himself to subdue us."

After a few hours, the storm abates. Only the rain continues to fall, slowly. The only sound is the heady patter of drizzle on the sodden ground—a whisper, a complaint. Those who are paying attention see the clouds rushing by, as if they were escaping toward a safer, more merciful sky. "The sky wants to wash the earth clean of all this horror," Bé mumbles, "but even the heavens can't do it."

The day goes by, and the noises of life trying to resurface can be heard: muffled words, children sobbing, the shrieks of startled birds. Toni comes back, proving Bé wrong.

"I'm going to be rude," she says, "and eat and run before it's too late or the wind starts blowing again. They say on the radio that the rain caused a lot of damage. Some of the houses in Bois de Chêne are flooded. Clara heard that after the rain, the women around here were drawing blackish, tarry water."

"Wouldn't we like to know, to understand why and how things work—" Bé starts to say, but her words are lost in in Toni's prattle.

I risk a glance outside. Behind the torn rags of the clouds, no one can see the gashes in the sky, the long slashes of the knives and the crimson trail.

Evening comes quickly. Down below, lights turn on and go off just as quickly. It's time to still the crying of children, and to cower, tiny and mute, in the darkness of our homes. Already the streets belong to the hunters.

JEANNE'S SEASON OF SORROW

TANTE BÉ PUTS A HAND ON HER CHEST, over her heart, as if to protect it. She comes here to get away, she tells me, not from the din of the city, but from the constant pull between the spiral of hell and daily life, the life that is no life at all. Bé lives with Jeanne—Jeanne who is locked up in unremitting sorrow. It gnaws at her. And she's so very old. Bé feels trapped, as if she's wedged in the neck of a bottle. The world is closing in around them, a little tighter each day. Of course, she knows what I've had to endure because of what I've said in public and in the paper. "I'm trading one sorrow for another," she says, "it's true, I know it. But, well...I have to live somewhere, and at least things are a bit calmer here. And I can afford to come: Jeanne's not alone, there are people who go visit her. Hortense never leaves her side, faithful as ever. Clarisse stops by all the time, even for a few minutes, and the twins too from time to time."

When she lived with us, Tante Bé couldn't stand to be around Charlot. Now that he's gone, she feels better coming here. She's happy that he left. And since she worries about me being alone, she takes it as her duty to keep me company.

Jeanne's only grandson, Richard, disappeared one afternoon on his way home from school. It happened just after the elections, and no one's heard from him since. People say they saw him get into a black unplated Vauxhall. In other words, he climbed into his coffin. The car belongs to a man named Romain, a born murderer. "You can see it in his eyes, his pupils," Bé says, "that bovine, callous, bloody look." Two other young men, student leaders, were taken too the same day as Richard, kidnapped by that werewolf on the road to Pétion-Ville.

After Richard disappeared, Jeanne went mad. "My life is a broken promise," she mutters day and night. And Richard was so promising, a brilliant student, barely twenty, about to start his second year of medical school, in a country where more than three-quarters of the population have never even laid eyes on a doctor.

Since Richard was kidnapped, Jeanne's life has been a dazed dance of questions, futile attempts and expectations and, above all, dashed hope. "As soon as she wakes up," Bé explains, "Jeanne starts imagining the day her boy will come back. She tells herself that he'll come back to us again, as if he'd never left, and everything in the house will be exactly as it was before."

She gets dressed and climbs the stairs, waiting on each step. Will her heart just stop beating all of a sudden? She drags her stiff limbs along, like wood against wood, scraping the old planks. She refuses help and does not want to be contradicted. Hortense can't do a thing about it. Jeanne goes up and down the steep stairs alone. A kind of calvary maybe? What reward does she expect at the end of the sacrifice, and from what god?

She's out of breath when she gets to the top, her foot finally on the last step. She doesn't move. She lays her hand on the banister. She turns the handle of Richard's bedroom door. What's left of Richard in her tattered memory? Vague images, the warmth of a playful voice? No one knows what to say or how to say it. Jeanne doesn't let anything in, nothing and no one can touch her sorrow. When at last she enters his room, all the sounds of the house and the outside world fade away. What does she do in there, in that room locked up like a sanctuary? Maybe she prays. She must be looking at photos, snapshots of a fading tenderness. After a long time, we think she's asleep, but then she begins to moan. And sob, and wail. Tears are all she has left. The cry is buried within her. It's blood-curdling, the keening of a body overwhelmed by pain, a body deserted, abandoned. Her whole world is wailing. Her whole world is a cry, the cry is her jailer and her prison.

When did she last eat? Has she slept? She doesn't really know. She's completely lost her bearings, except pain and weeping. Her grief is an axe plunged into her chest, its blows relentless. She is alive, but only to feel the barbs digging into her, far away, farther still. Her empty eyes, her dry lips, her whole being speaks only of an evil beyond words.

We tell ourselves that her sorrow, which expands day after day like a lake beneath her feet, will eventually submerge her entirely. We tell ourselves that at her age—she is three times thirty years old—she has nothing left to be waiting for. Yet she waits. Each day, like a speechless river, she slides across the immense desert her life has become. Her skinny legs, clad in funeral-black stockings, shuffle her to the bench under the almond tree. She waits. She looks at her hands, turns them, turns them over, and with a trembling finger traces the lines that might have foretold this season of despair.

Often, she counts on her fingers as she softly hums a lullaby from another time, the song popping up as if to taunt her memory cluttered by the echo of all that wailing. Sometimes she manages to walk to the bottom of the garden. She stretches out on the ground or curls up between the roots of a tree as if she wants to lose herself there, fall asleep forever. She collects small stones and counts the days, the seasons, the centuries of absence. She spends most evenings facing the front door, plucking a rosary mechanically, her dull eyes glued to the door. Time is no longer time, only cliffs and scree tumbling her dismembered life away.

She watched the child grow up after his mother died in childbirth. He was like a tree she had planted in the soil herself. She cared for him, loved him more than she'd ever thought it was possible to love. How many prayers, how many novenas to Mary Mother of God and of all men and women will bring the child back to her? The child is gone. The child whose voice she hears only in her dreams. Her child is gone and as an inheritance she has nothing but endless lament. In her old age, Jeanne has been orphaned of everything. Yet still she waits, in the unforgiving night. Sometimes she sits up, she comes back to life, as if in her nightmares the child has reappeared and he is there, standing before her. Inside the dream she opens her arms and listens, but all she can hear in the distance is the baying of dogs and the rhythmic pounding of soldiers' footsteps.

Bé's words make me weep. By the time she's done telling me the story she's crying too, and I comfort her like a child, cradling her against me. For some time now, she's been losing her grip on life. Often, her mind is far away. On the other hand, she has moments when she's completely lucid and claims she's rid herself of fear. Her lips are clamped together, her nostrils quivering. "There's no more room for weariness in this old woman's body," she cries, though I don't quite understand why. "You don't need to be a Marie-Jeanne, as they say, a warrior, to protect those who sprang from our loins."

BÉATRICE IMBERT

Bé's devotion to Jeanne and me is boundless. Bé is my mother's sister, the youngest of the three. Jeanne is the eldest. Bé raised Clarisse and me. She had been married for a few years but never had children. After my mother died in a stupid boating accident in Grand-Anse, Bé found herself with two daughters to raise.

Whatever her flaws, and despite the contradictions she'd absorbed from her environment, Bé wanted more than anything to teach us to live in the light, to stand up to cruelty. Yet even that—expecting respect, sometimes standing at all—is a struggle. And it was only possible through education, Bé told us. She was a feminist before her time. "Your first husband should be your diploma," she claimed. "There's no dignity without education." How could we know that dignity would be just a vague idea, an unattainable dream?

Everyone in the family said that Bé liked me best. According to Papa, I reminded Bé of her subversive side; he didn't say careless, but I'm sure he thought it. Bé, meanwhile, likes to repeat that I'm not afraid to grab the truth by the throat. "Mika, unlike Clarisse, never lies. She doesn't know how to cheat, she doesn't tell tales." "What she doesn't know," Clarisse tells me, "is how much you lie to yourself, my dear sister—about your idiot husband, among other things."

Bé took care of my children too. She only left when she realized that her rancour for their father, which grew as the years went by, was a source of acrimony that was hard to control. It was getting to be too much, according to her; she no longer even deigned to respond to Charlot's greetings.

What was the reason for Bé's open aversion to Charles-Émile? Nobody knew. When I asked her, she replied that there was nothing better than experience. "After knowing Benoît Cheminot, I only have to meet a man to know what he's made of."

Not many people remember that, for four years, which seemed like four centuries to her, Béatrice Imbert was married to Benoît Cheminot, a pharmacist who had a shop on Piquant. The pharmacy was huge—two storefronts, with a wide porch and a row of four double doors. You could come in through the first set of doors. The other side led to a bakery and a haberdashery with a sign that flashed cheerfully in the night, *Aux belles choses, chez Janine.* When locals went to the pharmacy, they referred to it as if it were Cheminot's own home, because he lived upstairs, over the store in the front part of the ground floor.

At the back of the building, there must have been a storage area and the area where the drugs and other products were prepared. The whole neighbourhood knew that the pharmacist strictly forbade his wife from leaving the house without him. Béatrice was his property. She existed to take care of him and his business and to run his household. Not only was he controlling, he also insulted her constantly. He accused her of sleeping with every man in town, though Cheminot himself was a lousy lay. From the very first day, Béatrice knew she was done for. She soon found out that Cheminot, a consummate hypocrite, had playboys all over town. Bé was seething. The man had married her for the sole purpose of keeping up appearances.

We couldn't believe it—our Bé, caught up in such drama? Unimaginable. Clarisse used to say that life has its mysteries, like these incomprehensible marriages. This one, in any case, had more than one person scratching their head. We sometimes saw the two of them together, the fat man trotting on his stubby little legs, carrying the pipe he sucked at all day long, and Béatrice trying to slow her stride to let him keep up with her.

Béatrice was a tall woman, strong, sturdy, even, with a very beautiful, symmetrical face. She had a plum complexion and shining almond-shaped eyes. Next to her, Benoît looked like a gnome, and a grumpy one to boot. The marriage was crushing for Béatrice, but by the time she figured it out, it was too late; the damage was done, and she would bear the scars forever. How could she forget, she said even now, the few times when she had tried to talk to Benoît or to get closer to him. He would bare his teeth at her, like an animal. He had the bad habit of flexing his jaw—"like a madman," Bé said. "And he had huge horse teeth! If he'd at least been handsome," she went on, "or good in bed..." "You're forgetting," Clarisse chuckled, "that he was especially gifted with men." Bé looked at us, taken aback. "It's true, my girl," she sighed, "I forget that. He had a lot of lovers...He was a disaster."

Like so many girls at the time, Bé had married the first man who came along. Were they trying to ease a burden on their families, did they want to escape how harsh family life could be for girls? Had they found what they believed was love, did they want a place of their own, where they could be in charge? Was it for sex, which for most young women was forbidden and mysterious? When we asked her, Bé didn't know what to say. We could tell that, like so many others, she had entered into marriage unflinchingly, with good intentions, as one might enter a convent.

One Saturday evening, Benoît Cheminot went out, as usual, without a word of explanation, and locked all the doors. Béatrice had gone more than a week without setting foot outside. *The man I married is keeping me here like a captive*, she said to herself, *with no chance of liberation. Why am I accepting this humiliation?* Benoît wouldn't be back until dawn, busy rolling around in some man's bed. And here she was endorsing this farce. *Haven't I lost enough? This loveless match has made me relinquish even the keys to my dreams.* It was time to salvage what could be.

Around four o'clock that morning, Benoît returned from his romp. He always came home looking dazed and depleted, as if he was under the effect of some drug, and smelling sour, the stench of alcohol and semen on his clothes and his skin. He tore off his clothes and flung them into the bedroom and ordered his wife to come wash him. That was their Sunday morning ritual. Without saying a word, Béatrice fetched a jug of warm water, a bowl, and a towel. She washed him, and Benoît was snoring before she'd even finished.

Around eleven o'clock, before Benoît woke up to demand lunch, Béatrice decided to go on the offensive. She came back to the bedroom holding a plastic bottle that contained a mixture she had prepared. Holding the bottle firmly, she walked up to the bed and looked at the man sleeping. The drums of revolt were beating in her head. Her arms shook, and she understood that there was fear there too, as well as rage. She struggled with herself; would her resolve weaken? Appealing to her bottomless well of silent determination—the same determination that had enabled her to endure nearly five years of suffering with this deceitful, disagreeable man—she took a deep breath. "Benny, Benny," she murmured.

Benoît Cheminot opened his eyes, furious, ready to spew insults or to hit his wife. But Bé's tone stopped him cold. He stared at her. She didn't even have to raise her voice.

"You will listen to me, to everything I have to say. I don't want to hear a single word from you. Your reign is over, Benoît Cheminot. I'm leaving. My suitcase is packed. If you make a move, I'll spray you with the contents of this bottle."

He looked around the room, distraught. Bé had to act quickly. She held the bottle up high, at the ready.

"I've learned enough over these four years with you to know by heart the whole repertoire of hate. But I've also learned how to mix the most abominable poison—here, in this bottle. One drop on your skin and you're done. There's enough in here to wipe you out and all your children and your children's children."

Benoît struggled to keep his composure.

"Don't talk nonsense!" he said, trying to sound threatening.

"Shut up!" Béatrice replied. "I will never know what made you what you are, and I don't care. But I want to tell you that I got myself a gun and will have it with me at all times from now on. The day you get in my way, I will shoot you. I also have gasoline, paper, matches, and kindling, and if I hear so much as the squeak of your footsteps, if you come after me, I will set fire to this house without a moment's hesitation. All that will be left of you will be fat dribbling into the gutter."

Bé backed out of the room. She pulled the door closed and left the house.

◆

Bé never let anyone get away with anything. She was intent on learning; she read a lot and subscribed to several journals and magazines. She knew she had a duty to arm herself because life had dropped two girls in her arms, two orphans to raise. How many times had she told us the story of her life? Her gaze faraway, seeing what only she could really see, Bé wove a whole landscape for us. She tried to be calm and serene, though as always what she'd lived through and what she'd had to do to protect herself gave Bé's words an edge. Her stare was icy. "This is what I've gotten from men, their legacy," she cried. She wasn't afraid of shocking anyone. She'd lived through hell, she said, and she would rather go broke buying up all the dildos on earth—she had a whole collection, she claimed, and had named each one—than bring the fickleness of an actual, two-legged man into her bed. "It's all right from time to time," she added, oblivious to our shock. "But leaving my desire and my pleasure permanently in the hands of a man—never! And for tenderness, I have you," she winked. I knew she was looking at me, too, thinking of my marriage to Charlot. I dropped my head. She smiled sadly, a smile that faded right away in the mist of memory.

WOMEN DISMANTLED

I HAD A LONG CONVERSATION this morning with Clarisse. She's worried about Bé and Jeanne's health.

"They're getting old, both of them, Mika," she tells me, her voice quavering. "I can feel them falling away a little bit more each day, a little bit faster. Bé is fading, lost in the silence she's gathered around herself. Now…I wonder if it could be dementia. We can't pretend not to see it. And Jeanne, who's buried in her grief. I try to spend time with Jeanne every day, but it's so depressing, Mimi, the way she's just letting herself slip away. When she has company, she comes out of it a little, but every day, after I see her, I go home thinking tomorrow she'll be gone. Her sorrow is enormous."

"What we have to understand, Clarisse, darling, is that they're both really old, as you've just said yourself, and that they've been through more than a lifetime's worth of grief this past year. Jeanne will never recover from Richard's disappearance."

On Sunday, at noon, we all get together, the whole family. "Picking up where life left off," Clarisse says. We're at Jeanne's house for lunch with the children. Sonia and Maria seem worried. Félix, who's always taciturn, didn't stick around to chat, he just ate and then went off by himself to read his book. I was having coffee, sitting between Jeanne and Bé, when he came back toward us. I could tell he was flustered; he's never been clingy. For the first time since this all started, he asked me what was going on at the newspaper, why I kept going. I don't see the DKWs as much up near the house, I answer him, and I hardly ever go in to the office anymore. In any case, I'm so preoccupied with so many things that I can't write. My latest article on the Ganthier murders, and the other one, on land reform, which I finally finished, are still waiting to be published.

Clarisse sings as she tends to Jeanne's plants, which are dying too. Her gravelly voice has always annoyed Félix. When's our life going to go back to normal, he asks me. He's fifteen, he obviously needs to be at home. For a second I doubt myself, I feel guilty: what should I be doing for my children?

"I would so much like to be able to answer you properly, Félix. You just have to be patient."

Here, like this, around the children, I feel like I've lost control. For the past few months, my life has been limited to this insane back and forth between Jeanne and Bé. Once more, here I am, sitting between two old women who are riffling through their troubles. When I'm with them, I try to read to pass the time, especially old classics. I always read the same books, probably because it requires less effort. And I have the stubborn impression—it must come from Bé, her obsession for knowledge and the written word, which she passed on to us—that I'm going to discover something significant in these books, some timeless truth allowing me to better understand the unfathomable events unfolding around me.

I've grabbed a battered copy of Marivaux's *Slave Island*, and I flip through the book as we talk. I'm sure Clarisse will make fun of me, as she does, for what she calls my archaic reading material. Marivaux wrote his utopia in 1725, she will snipe. *Just look at the state of the world, and draw your own conclusions!*

I watch Jeanne, small and wrinkled in her armchair. Her eyes are glued to Félix, who must remind her of Richard. She is shivering despite the heat, draped in shawls and blankets as if the folds of the familiar cloth might hold some comfort that's not really there. I take her hands in mine. They're cold. I can feel her bones, as if the flesh is getting thinner every day. Jeanne hardly eats anymore. I understand: Bé suffers so much, watching her sister let herself go, gently—locked up inside her cry, as she says. Although, when you listen closely, you realize that Jeanne is occasionally completely rational. She turns to me suddenly. "Why don't we get to have a normal life? Aren't we entitled to live far and free from all this sadness?"

On the sidewalk, a young girl hurries by. The clacking of her heels catches Jeanne's attention. She lifts her head and glances at the girl with something akin to compassion, as if remembering that another world exists, ailing outside these walls. Jeanne leans toward me and pulls my arm to bring me closer.

"See that girl, there?" she whispers. "Look at the way she walks, all bent over, she's almost a hunchback. That's Marie Nina, Ismène's daughter. She was born in the neighbourhood, we knew her growing up, remember? Look at her now, how crooked she is. Everything is too heavy for us now. They say her boss forces her to sell herself to keep her job. Can you believe that?"

Her eyes well up.

"She can't be more than eighteen years old, you know," Jeanne continues. "Barely eighteen! What a tragedy this is, Mimi. But she can't do anything, poor girl, they're too powerful. Ismène, the mother, doesn't work anymore. She can't work. It was so hard for her to set up her business when she was selling sewing notions; it was blood, sweat, and tears, truly. When she got sick, she lost everything. It was serious; she had a heart attack, just like that. She was forced to close down, and she went bankrupt. Now Ismène's husband, André—he was a mason or a painter, I don't remember—disappeared, after an altercation at the seaside with a man called Éloïs Maître. That's what people say. That Éloïs Maître fellow, who was a baker, closed his bakery to join the assassins. Now he shares the same trough as the monster who's president. What times we live in! Poor thing," Jeanne sighs. "Now she has to take care of the whole family. She has a whole pile of little brothers and sisters."

Jeanne closes her eyes for a moment, relaxes, and opens them again. She looks at me as if she were waiting for a word to come, for some light. I don't say anything. She presses herself against me, her nails, her bony fingers clasping my skin, a reminder of her despair. The shawls are thick. Her heart is beating, fighting for her.

I look at her closely. Time is passing much more quickly for her than for me. Has she already crossed over? I still see a sparkle in her eyes that reminds me of my mother. Could it be that, as we stand together, our breath mingling, she's thinking of her too—her sister, a part of her, the woman I look almost exactly like, who was gone so young, too soon? Jeanne is closer now to Maman than I am. Although—given the cannibalistic wind blowing relentlessly, how can we guess what each day holds? Tears run silently down Jeanne's furrowed cheeks. A moment later, she leans over to me.

"When I don't have the strength to scream, I weep." Her voice is like a child's. "I have to scream, Mimi, do you understand? Silence is much worse than what I've suffered. Ever since they took him away from me, I've been screaming every day. I have nights and days full of screaming in my guts. Screaming is the only way I can go on. I would never have thought that at the end of my life I would have become nothing but screaming—the cry of a woman without a name, a decaying carcass. Bé scolds me when I say this, but what else am I? My name, my child, my innards have been fed to the pigs. I am a woman in ruins. I am nothing. I am nothing," Jeanne repeats. "But every night, I dream the same dream: the one where fear has crossed over to the other shore, the face of fear has changed."

◆

Bé always gets up early in the morning. Back when she still lived with me, she would get up before dawn and head down to the garden. Eventually, the children would go find her, disturbing her peace and quiet and her endless soliloquies, but in the morning, barefoot, her hair down, she walked in the garden, one hand holding the hem of her nightgown, already soaked by dew. She rubbed dew on her face too; she said it was good for the skin. She doesn't go down to the garden any more. Now she stands on the porch stairs. I understand why she's afraid. After all, they threw that stone under my window. I'm still shaken. Every day since Bé came back, I find her on the stoop, motionless, frozen in time. She can spend hours looking out, without seeing the mass of people pouring down to the bottom of the hill, on the path that is always the same, though now the light is joyless, even at dawn.

Her eyes are distant and she rubs at her fingers, small circular motions, as if she were giving herself a massage. But I know that she's counting too, like Jeanne, counting the weeks, the months, the days spent under siege, and the sleepless nights since Richard was taken. She's sworn that she'll still be counting in her coffin if he hasn't come back by the time she's gone.

This morning, as she peers at the lines of her dry hands, following a trail of veins, she turns around, staring at me with her grey eyes.

"Look!"

I turn my head but I don't see anything. There's nothing but the path down the hill and the anonymous silhouettes.

"Look," she says again.

She blinks rapidly, as if she has a tic.

"The children used to play there in the morning. Do you remember? In the garden. In the morning. Richard, Soledad and the others. Look. They're not there anymore, are they? There's nothing left but tears. In my head, everywhere, sobbing. You can hear them, can't you? This town is going to vanish, they're going to devour everyone down to the last sob."

From the pocket of her bathrobe, she takes out a small metal box, its green paint peeling. She opens the tin carefully, as if she were afraid that the contents might evaporate. Her trembling fingers awkwardly shape two greyish cotton-wool plugs. Mumbling, she wedges them into her ears as best she can. "I don't want to hear any more…No more."

At the edge of nothingness, in the deepest part of all that is intolerable, through Bé the demented world resounds.

THE SIEGE

THE ARTICLE ON GANTHIER was finally published yesterday. *Virulent and partisan*, according to a journalist at *La Voix du Nord,* a radio station on the Duvalier payroll. Salnave called to inform me that Colonel Sony Borges himself had phoned the newspaper to hurl abuse at me.

"He wanted to talk to you. You weren't there, so he spoke to the director. Everybody at the newspaper is terrified."

"So the famous Colonel Borges called the newspaper. How odd: he could just as easily have come to my house, what with the goons up the street who've invaded the neighbourhood again. They've taken up permanent residence. Yesterday I counted four cars hidden in the trees. I can't just run off into the mountains! The colonel knows where to find me."

"We'll have to be more careful, Mika."

Another night of terror. Salnave told me this was coming, in a way. The nighttime phone calls started again. I spend the morning hiding in my room with the shutters closed. I'm chugging herbal tea, soursop and lemon balm. I sneak into Bé's room.

"Believe me if you want," she says to me in a low voice. "They want to scare us but they're the ones who are shaking every night despite the absurd number of weapons they have stored under their beds. They draw their strength only from our faithlessness, Mimi, I'm telling you. And they're afraid all the same."

"But they have professionals backing them up, Bé, they have help, you know. American soldiers, French gendarmes from Melun.

They're up on all the new means of repression. They don't have to be afraid. Certainly they're less afraid than we are."

It's going to be a long day. I can't shake the sound of the children when they were young enough to have fun in the garden, that vision. I used to watch them playing in the yard from the window while Bé looked after them.

My prayer this morning to a deaf, blind god: *Keep me from all the tangled whispers, from these terrified voices.* But it's no use. These rumours about the death squads and the persecution seeps into everything now, the forever awful news are part of my world, they invade my space day after day. Relentless, like wardens, standing guard all around me.

Bé and I are having breakfast outside after she asked why we were hiding in the house. "It's pointless. We're in prison no matter where we go in this country!"

◆

Since the beginning of the siege, I've spent countless hours going over the situation, and I still can't see a way out, no matter how I look at it. I would have liked to have been able to talk to Soledad about this. She's sharp and rational, and I often rely on her insights. Soledad, who decided at the age of nineteen to leave. From childhood she'd dreamed of spreading her wings, she said—somewhere else, toward the multiple lives she has led since she left—philosophy, dance, painting, so many other wonders.

When the phone rings, I'm stunned to hear Soledad on the other end of the line. Soledad, doing her best to pretend she's not worried. She's coming tomorrow, she's on her way. For a second I'm unable to speak.

"Can you hear me? Mama, can you hear me?" she calls, full of apprehension.

I'm torn between yearning for the presence of my beloved child and the danger from which I must protect her. I have to keep her from coming.

"No, Soledad," I stammer, "that's not possible! There's no freedom at all, there's no way through."

"I know, Mama, I know everything."

Before I come to my senses—click. The earth opens up beneath my feet, and I slide toward the abyss.

How does she know, what does she know? I don't recognize my own voice. I hear awful squeaks, little high-pitched cries. Where are they coming from? My chest? What a mess, good lord. I get up. My back is stiff, and I'm suddenly so cold. I pace nervously around the room, then I go hide in the study.

Should I call Charlot and demand that he intervene, call Soledad, order her not to come? This is going to end badly. Soledad can't come back! I have to change her mind, to prevent her from coming here, no matter what. Things are getting worse: after the scandalous celebrations on October 22, all those who'd been brought from the countryside to boost the numbers were released all over the city. They sleep in the bushes, on people's doorsteps, like animals. Some are breaking into people's houses, they have guns.

Yesterday I had to go into town to renew a prescription. Valium for Bé, who isn't sleeping at all. While I was talking to the pharmacist, a truck came racing down the narrow street and pulled up in front of the pharmacy, screeching its tires. The pharmacist tipped my tablets into the bottle. She had to start again, her hands were shaking so hard: she'd seen the men come in. The pills clattered on the metal counter; she counted them out again, and again they fell. Finally she slid the cork in the bottle, handed me the bag, and told me to come pay another time. I walked out of the pharmacy, my pulse buzzing in my temples, though the hum couldn't drown out the beastly growls. One of the men went up to the counter, as his cronies—armed, of course—looked on. Behind the counter, the poor woman looked like she was about to pass out. "You old bitch," the man barked at her, "can't you see that your pills haven't done anything for me? This sick thing you see here between my legs, well, I can make you eat it or shove it up your fat ass if you don't give me some medication right away!"

Apparently, poor madame Dulot doesn't dare close her pharmacy, she's too worried about what they might do to retaliate. Every day, they come, grab something and leave without paying. The whole gang is trying to get to her husband, Ernest Dulot, who's wanted by the squad bosses—Simon, Bertrand, Gracia, and Delva, Lolo something or other, and two others named Désinor and Novembre. They were all there yesterday, in the truck, around the corner. By rue Chaumont, near Jeanne's place, the terrace of the Petit Café des Amis was crowded with armed men, their eyes hidden behind dark glasses. Noisy and reeking of alcohol, they were shouting at the top of their lungs, slamming dominos on the tables psychotically and passing around flasks full of rum. They say the café owner, Jean Toussaint, a peaceful man and father of five, was thrown in prison and murdered. Music in honour of the tyrant poured out of the café windows, poisoning the street and the whole neighbourhood.

CLARISSE'S FURY

CLARISSE AND I ARE DRIVING TO THE AIRPORT. She is smoking one cigarette after another, swearing like a sailor as she swerves to avoid the potholes. Over and over, I recite the same poem again, Rilke. I'm crying; since I found out that Soledad was coming home I've done nothing but cry.

There they live, like blossoms white and pale
and, amazed at the hard world, they die.
And no one sees the gaping grimace
that leaves the smile of a tender race
disfigured in nameless nights.

"Do you know, Mika," Clarisse says to me out of nowhere, "that the monsters who are in power have been intercepting people as they get off the plane? Most of them have never been released."

I don't react.

"They have a copy of the manifest, and an army officer checks off the passengers' names as they get off the plane. Anyone coming from Europe, especially Eastern Europe, is detained. If at least Charles-Émile had deigned to come with you...Because of him, now we're going to land right in the cesspool of criminals the airport has become. I suppose he had an excellent excuse for not coming to welcome his daughter, as always, didn't he? If anyone touches a single hair on Soledad's head, he'll have to deal with me," she spits, her voice distorted by fear and fury.

This is what I was dreading, I think while Clarisse gabbles on; she's going to complain about Charlot the whole way there. I close my eyes, but Clarisse pesters me, her voice like a stubborn insect. My silence offends her, and she doubles down: "Mika, you've always been like this! You say one thing and do another. Haven't you ever stopped to wonder why?"

Clarisse punctuates her scathing proclamations with a godawful kissing of her teeth, which has always driven Bé around the bend (when we were young, Bé told Clarisse it was the height of vulgarity). I don't know what Clarisse is talking about, and I don't want to know. I think about seeing Soli, whom I haven't seen for two years, and I try to stay calm. My sister's words come back to me now in a fog, where politics, personal relationships, and emotions are all mixed up. I should have gone to the airport alone, or else asked Salnave or maybe Jean-François. I'm kicking myself for not having thought this through. Have I always depended on Clarisse?

The sun is shy today, only a thin glowing film sits over the horizon. But no matter how brightly it shines, it can't hide the menace that surrounds us, it can't make us forget the terror that is everywhere, spreading like the destruction all around us: concrete, asphalt, torn-down buildings, mountains of garbage, putrid smells, and stray dogs, mangy and starving, dogs full of ticks scratching themselves furiously in the middle of the road, and the clamour, human anthills, dense smoke, sirens, greyish trees covered in thick yellow dust, and in every corner, predators lying in wait.

We watch the people going by: they're tired of fighting, tired of being constantly harassed by the pack.

"Have they just decided to sink into this misery forever?" Clarisse grumbles, finally changing the subject.

"What else can they do, locked up on this island?"

"Every night boats are leaving, loaded with peasants fleeing atrocities and murders, running away from the gangsters who are trying to confiscate their land. It's happening now. It's always happened here. Other beasts replace those that came before, and on and on. And then there's us, like animals. Hunted."

"Must we pave the ocean with bobbing dinghies full of refugees so that the killing finally stops, and we have peace?"

"We'd only be feeding the sharks. And those who survive the crossing end up rotting in concentration camps in the United States. Imagine the arrogance: even today, those reprobates are still lynching negroes. They're the same men who landed in this country in 1915 to enslave us and force us to bow down before them—wi bwana, wi misye blan."

"You're forgetting that we are the ones who are primarily responsible for this situation. We put Duvalier in power."

"No need to remind me!" she breaks in. "But they've been fucking up the whole time! And you're forgetting that the balance of power is so unequal that we don't stand a chance."

She lets loose a peal of laughter, the way she does, which scares the bejesus out of me. And doesn't let me get a word in edgewise: "We forced those hired guns to go back to their country; do you really think they'll ever forgive us? Squatting there on all their riches, with nothing to do all day long but shit on the rest of the world—and believe me, they do it gladly. They're the same as the French, how many times do I have to tell you? Don't you remember everything they did to us here before they left? Have you forgotten that they killed Péralte, then Batraville, who were fighting against the occupation in this country? Péralte was murdered by the sergeants Henneken and Button, and they were rewarded for the assassination! Péralte's corpse was gibbeted on a cross—as a symbol, powerful and persistent. And the purpose of the demonstration?"

"To show us that as masters of the world they were going to make us to carry the cross! I know the chorus, darling."

"Well, you—As a journalist, that's what you should be writing about."

Clarisse doesn't think too highly of me working at the newspaper. I don't blame her. In the end, it's her impatience with the state of the country—her legitimate impatience—that makes her so baleful. As usual, I turn a deaf ear.

"It's true that Péralte was murdered by the Americans," I say at last. "What's also true is that they would undoubtedly have killed him one way or another. But he was betrayed by one of his officers, Jean-Baptiste Conzé, who guided the Marines to his hideout. Making us out to be victims doesn't serve our cause, you know that as well as I do. All it does is reinforce a collective exculpation."

"We've been so busy defending ourselves with whatever scant means we have that we've never had time to build a nation for ourselves. How can we survive in a sea full of sharks? We don't even have a voice! We haven't had a voice since—"

"Maybe one day we'll get back the voice that was silenced," I sigh.

We cross a canal. Muddy water trickles beneath the rickety bridge, and animals and people wade about. On the left, a maze of alleys has taken over a small hill. Other alleyways, dug right into the ground, run almost to the top. There, in the slums, flimsy shacks are perched so high it's like they've been hooked in the sky on an invisible thread.

◆

The airport is crowded, hot, and humid. The plane is late. Clarisse can't stand still. The atmosphere is unbreathable. There is only room for assassins: soldiers, the death squads and their American and French advisors, and other puppets. The parking lot is packed with death cars: Citroën DS, Mercedes 220, Vauxhall, Jeeps. Clarisse stomps around, complaining about the heat. She's thirsty, she looks like she's about to cry, and I'm praying, begging all the saints in heaven. I dread Clarisse's outbursts more than anything else in the world. *Not now*, I tell myself, *I can't deal with it*. The loudspeakers crackle grimly: a plane has landed. Soon Soli will be here.

ONE LAST TIME

NOVEMBER AND DECEMBER ARE SAD and so dark, despite the ever-present sun. The only thing that brings some light into my life is having Soledad here—Soli Jolie, as Bé calls her. As I'd anticipated, as soon as his sister arrived, Félix decided he was no longer staying with Clarisse. Soon the girls will come too, surely. The house is a little more lively, and I can hardly complain; my seclusion has gone on long enough. With Soli, I try to pick up where we left off, to make up for the days and months I've missed in her life, if I can. Being a mother can be so fraught. These past two years have been up taken by my work at the Women's League for the Right to Vote, then these elections and what's come after—the maelstrom that's taken over my life…All of it pulled me away from Soledad.

She was disappointed that I didn't come to Granada this year to visit her, as I'd promised I would. I find out about Javier, who's come into her life, more or less between the lines—in how she looks away and the fullness on her face when she says his name.

"Does he have a last name? Is it more than a fling?" I tease her.

She pouts. Can love really last, she asks me.

"The love I have for you will last a lifetime."

Félix, who hasn't left Soledad's side since her return, shuffles closer. He loops his arms around her neck. Félix has a million questions: What sports does Javier like? What's he studying at university? Will he visit Haiti?

"We're not there yet. Not yet, not yet." Soledad runs away.

"I'm not prepared for all these things mothers need to know, what we need to do, to tell our children, in order to support them," I confide in Clarisse one evening. Soledad has come back to me as a woman, and in love, and I am at a loss.

"It's something to be happy about, Mika! She's growing up fast, it's true. I've been thinking about her a lot since I saw her, how strong she is, headstrong. You don't need to worry about her. She would have withered away here. Soli can turn the most banal bit of nothing into a miracle. She's a fine woman, there isn't an ounce of vulgarity in her."

"My problem is that her life is moving forward so fast, at a pace even she can't control. She's going back to Granada at the end of January. She'll have her classes. And on top of school she'll be performing in a new production of *Yerma*."

"What's the problem? Soledad's been able to not get bogged down. She's not afraid to explore, to go beyond the limits you and I have always imposed on ourselves."

"You're right, Clarissa, darling. It's all jumbled—the future of children in this country, the country itself. We're adrift, and there's no end in sight. Félix sometimes seems so depressed and I can sense his anxiety about the situation I'm in. He has no prospects. And now Soledad. When I see her, I feel like I held the most beautiful butterfly in the palm of my hands, and it's flown away."

"It's a beautiful image, Mika. You should celebrate her flight. The butterfly flies up, it doesn't sink down into the depths. There's something euphoric about it. It's not sad, there's nothing to be anxious about, my dear sister."

Around mid-December, Jeanne's two dogs were found dead in the garden. What indescribable sorrow when I go to her house and they don't come running at me, tongues hanging out, their wet noses. I miss their humanity, their affection. Jeanne has grown so weak that it doesn't even occur to her to ask what's become of the dogs she loved so much. Or maybe she knows and says nothing.

Toni doesn't come up to see us anymore, so Soledad and I went to visit her. The fear is everywhere in her house, like a presence, lurking in the corners, watching her. Her eyes dart around the room as she flicks through her rosary, her private recitation. All her serenity, all her courage seems to have ebbed away. I ask her what's going on, why she's so disoriented. She takes me by the hand and leads me to her bedroom. There, she opens a closet and pulls me inside.

"A black Vauxhall has been parked out front every night for the past two weeks. Yesterday, during the night, I felt like there was someone in the hallway. And this morning, under my window, I found a stone painted with blood and tar. I dug a hole and buried it there." She crosses herself. Purple hollows under her eyes make the gleam of panic stand out all the more.

"It all started the day my son sent a man packing. He'd come to recruit him for the makout. The recruiter, a fellow named Abel Jérôme, was so cocky that he arrived with a package under his arm—the blue and red uniform, a wide-brimmed kepi, dark glasses, and two red scarves. Emilio told him to get out or he was going to smash out all his teeth with his hammer. The same day, Emilio was forced to shut up his shop and flee who knows where. The car has been parked at our door since, every night. It started the day after this thing with Emilio."

Her eyes are wide with terror. Toni looks like a madwoman.

"Is Emilio going to end up on one of those death boats to the United States?" she asks me.

I lead her out of the closet and join Soledad. She looks at Toni, her jaw tense. "If this goes on," she says once we've left the house, "Toni is going to sink. Can't you see how scared she is? It can't go on like this, she's going to get sick."

We only venture outside once a day, between four and five in the afternoon, when the streets are still full of people—hopefully the crowds offer some protection—or else early in the morning, to run a few quick errands. At that hour, we tell ourselves, the predators haven't yet taken up their posts at the corners, under the awnings and in the bushes, ready to pounce.

The newspaper is still publishing. Several of my colleagues are risking their lives. The publisher is asking us to keep a low profile, an editorial policy most journalists find difficult to follow. I flat-out refuse. I refuse silence, too.

I did everything I could to keep Soledad from coming up to the house with me. She'd be safer in town, at Jeanne's. But nothing I can say can convince her. "I came back to this country to be with you," she replied the last time I suggested that she move in with Jeanne.

◆

This morning, in Place Boyer, a brute named Gérard Louis, along with two others, William Régala and Emmanuel Orcel, burst into a man's house and dragged him into the street. The victim was shouting. "Tell me," he yelled to the people standing in the street, "tell me, what colour is the assassins' blood? It's time for us to find out! When will we finally see their blood spilled?" The man refused to be quiet. They tried to force him into their van. In the end, they shot him in the middle of the street. The three vampires unloaded their weapons into his body. I'm sure they'll leave him for the flies, for days. There have been so many lives shattered in this place, with its fallow heart—fallow since the country was born. When will the island be fertile, in how many years? Where is hope hiding?

It's already January second. The twins came up to see us shortly before Christmas. They've decided that they're going to stay here with Soledad and me too. They won't leave—not until those cars stop going up and down the road, they say. We hear them in the night—the hunters, making their weapons sing.

I spoke to Bé this morning. Like Jeanne, she's becoming less coherent. "Yesterday afternoon," she tells me, "I went to the bazaar." I don't know what she's talking about, and I didn't want to ask her what bazaar she was talking about. Maybe she wanted to tell me another one of her nerve-racking dreams. "I was going back and forth in the bazaar," she says. "There were a lot of people despite the rain. People were puttering around as if they'd been waiting for the rain to wash themselves. But there was nothing to buy. All the stalls were empty, completely bare. People came and went, strolling up and down the aisles as if to say, *We're alive, we're here.*"

I'm trying to find a way into Bé's mind, but there's no key. Twice this morning, I asked her about Jeanne. Jeanne has hardly gotten out of bed since Christmas, yet Bé tells me she's gone to the Dessalines Barracks to meet the colonel.

"She wants to tell him that it's time to hand over the child they're keeping in prison! And we decided, Jeanne and I," she continues, "that if her child doesn't come back after this, we'll both go, we'll go together to the barracks, and we're going to slit the colonel's throat."

This situation with Jeanne and Bé upsets me; it can't go on any longer. Every day I spend hours listening to Bé tell me her nightmares. She believes they're real. Her whole life now revolves around the colonel.

I have to call the doctor tomorrow.

I spent a terrible night on the phone with Bé trying in vain to calm her down. She refused to go to bed until she had told me about her imaginary escapade to Dessalines Barracks, and she was crying so hard that Hortense had to call me. I begged Bé to wait until the next day, we could talk tomorrow, go back to bed, but she was adamant, and I had to hear the disconcertingly precise details of her supposed visit to the colonel.

"I turned the handle and slowly pushed open the door to the vestibule. Holding my breath, I stopped, listened. I walked into a large room full of desks. I looked around and saw something that looked like a machete leaning against an old cabinet. I tiptoed over and took the machete without hesitating for a second, but I realized the weapon was much too heavy. It would have been of no use to me. I opened another door. The colonel was there. I swear, he was afraid because he saw I was so determined. I said to him, 'Listen, Colonel, from here, from where I stand, here on the far shore of life, all the landscapes blur into one. But I know how to spot the monsters. They have the law on their side, they feel powerful; they walk around in broad daylight with their faces uncovered. Some choose crime, and that's their business. I am not here to negotiate for the redemption of hardened men, nor to plead for the redemption of a barren conscience. I have come for the child who sleeps in my soul, the one who has never left me. He alone has led me here. I am the unpleasant surprise, I am the thing you'd like to cross off your list. But it won't work, Colonel! At my age, I can be whatever I want to be because I'm no longer really here. These are not my own words, this is the language of the great hourglass. I am not of your world, Colonel. In my world there is no such thing as destiny. There's no apprehension, no pretense. That's why I was able to drag myself here, in search of the child, the child your men took away in the black Vauxhall. We are waiting for him, Jeanne and I, before we go. You see, we have already both crossed over.'

"'There are mothers who live in a dream,' I said, before turning my back on him, 'hoping against hope for the fruit of their womb to be reborn, to live again. And there is me, Béatrice Imbert. Don't ask me how I was able to reach your haven here, Colonel,' I shouted. 'You will never know!'"

Bé's voice went up a notch, and she started to cough. I said nothing. I could hear Hortense sighing in the background.

"'I have come, Colonel,'" Bé went on, "'only to tell you that I have already suffered all the abuse, I have known all the pain and overcome it, I have fought all the wars. As I stand before you, I have nothing more to lose. I have sold everything, bought everything, my bags are packed. I am only waiting for the return of the child.'

"Mimi, he could see the determination in my eyes, he could see my mettle. I swear to you, he was stunned. He didn't say a word. My girl, my little girl, you know there is no one more cowardly, more lily-livered than these murderers. I stared at him straight, and I could see the panic about to wash over him. For a moment he felt totally exposed, I'm telling you."

We have to see about getting Bé to take other medication. Valium's not enough. I'm sure she's going to say no. I don't know how to reach her. I don't have the key.

———◆———

Charlot called today. His daughters are refusing to talk to him, and he blames me for his children's attitude. He is their father, after all, he claims; they owe him respect. "Respect is not a duty," Sonia replied, "respect is earned." I stayed out of it. For a moment, as the children bickered like they used to, everything was fine and only remnants of fear lingered in my exhausted mind.

A fleeting, possible happiness. I stay to watch, in the evening, as the children play cards or dominoes, hiding in the bedroom. It's as though we were waiting for the wind of woe to change its course, to leave us be, to let our family live out its story outside of this nightmare. Sometimes I look in the mirror, my face wizened and washed out, and I don't recognize myself. My hair has gone white so quickly. Every night I dream the same dream, a portent of some calamity I can't see. I'm rambling; I'm obsessed by this dream. It's always the same, the same series of scenes in the same order.

First, childhood. I'm about ten years old. I'm lying up on the gallery, reading. I read everything, I love books. A jaundiced old woman emerges behind me. I don't know who she is, I can't quite make out her features, they are constantly changing. Instinctively, I put the book away, and then I shove my hands in my mouth, which bulges like a balloon. My fingers hurt, but I don't really understand why. Do my fingers know what's coming, do they sense the butchers' wrath? Words tumble from the old woman's mouth like sleet. Razor-edged words. *That's enough reading! We need you in the kitchen!* Her stare is relentless, her eyes tarnished by something unfulfilled. She glares daggers at me, and they pierce me to the marrow. The woman is yellow, she sputters, suffocating under the weight of her indignation. *Mika has committed a book!* she shouts, spinning around like a top. Words slip between her lips, she spits them out, hunching her shoulders and wincing from the effort. She curls her lip to reveal her incisors, like a dog. She whistles, grinding her molars, and brings her hand to her chest. In her poisonous voice, she warbles, *In the beginning, she used to write furtively, in the middle of the night, by candlelight.* Her voice is bile and rage. She lifts an emaciated finger like a blade and points to me. *As soon as she knew how to put the words together, she started to lie, she lies like she breathes, and over the years, she began to invent stories by the thousands, tall tales, lies. We thought one day she would come to reason, that these delusions would vanish in time. Alas, no. She is so stubborn.*

 A man starts to speak. I don't know him. He pretends to be my husband, I don't know. He could be my father, a cousin, an uncle, or a neighbour. It doesn't matter, only the voice matters—a voice that believes what it's saying, dripping with conviction, sincere and measured. *She is altogether abnormal*, the voice explains angrily, *she goes from being in a daze, long periods of apathy and painful waiting, to an obscure madness. Night and day, alone in her room, she scratches up sheaves of paper. It would take a powerful drug indeed to free her senses and her soul. She has lost her sense entirely.* Suddenly another man gets up and starts to moan. *Help her! She must be suffering, she must be ill...I know it, I feel it, I swear it...*

 The interrogation is vicious. The judge doesn't have a face. His head is an enormous ball. I can't see his eyes or his mouth, but I can hear his voice, thunderous and mechanical. Standing before him, I press my hands together to concentrate, try to forget the whiny excuses of tremulous milksops. And resist—resist the cold, such a weary cold, weeping through the walls of the interrogation room, which smells like dust, old papers, and grimy gowns. Cold fear, making its way through me. My statement, practised at length, comes out confused. The mob has plugged a tube from my brain to the maw of an old woman, and she drinks me, sucks me dry, she empties me. She drinks me in as she scowls, her nostrils quivering with hate. She will drink all of me, sucking me to the last word. Once more, the man points at me with his index finger. I begin to scream. *Resist the excision!*

I am speaking, and I resist the way you resist the pain of childbirth. There is chaos on my tongue, chaos in my belly, but the words come out. They have to come out, otherwise my life has no meaning. But the words are lawless. The mob growls to cover the sound of my voice. Still I speak, and once more I scream. *Refuse to be silenced!*

Amid the damnation of eyes upon me, I find that all I have are my mangled words. Alone with the hunters, the executioners, the inquisitors, the ideologues, the hecklers, the gravediggers. The judge bangs his gavel as hard as he can, demanding quiet, but the words continue to simmer in my head, and my temples, they rattle around in my guts, in my mouth. My voice refuses to be held captive, it explodes and I speak, convinced that the words are rising from the ground into me, they are rising from earth soaked in blood, the blood of the silenced masses. And I cry, *I am a tree of words*! I carry the words, all the words they refuse to hear. There is a price on my head, I know. I imagine my head rolling in the street, in a froth of blood. The predators kick it along, bouncing it on their toes like a stone. The satisfaction of having done their duty. The mob screams, *Whosoever has sinned shall pay!* But before that I will speak, I will say everything. That's when the man, the father or husband, the voice of absolute certainty, declares, *Every book Mika has written shall be burned. I will see to it myself!* He will see to it himself. The books will be burned. So shall it be. The judge nods the globe of his head. A bell tolls and the room shudders. A whisper shivers through the crowd. The judge stands, extends a vengeful hand toward me, and proclaims, *You wanted to change the world. For this you shall be condemned to silence and oblivion. You will be buried alive.*"

The bell tolls one last time.

THE ATTACK

I AM WITH MY CHILDREN and I have barely finished telling them the dream when it happens. We didn't hear the crunch of tires. Did they walk up the hill? It doesn't matter. That night, on the night of January 5, 1958, they lead us into an abyss that devours us, even our screams.

Soledad has brought the hot kettle to the table. We are about to drink another cup of lemon balm tea. Félix and his sisters have gone upstairs to play cards. Soli goes to the back door to let in some air. It's so hot. We rarely use the back terrace, though it's larger and nicer than the one at the front of the house, because it opens onto wild, scrubby bushes. It's long since been abandoned to the neighbourhood's stray cats.

That's how they come in.

When she opens the door, Soledad realizes that the rain has puddled here and there on the cement slabs. "We should wipe all this up before someone slips and falls," she says. She walks down the stairs, and standing on tiptoe, stretches her arms up to reach the mop that's hanging on the wall. She stands back down, and that's when she hears them in the bushes. In the half light, slowly, they move forward.

After the evening prayer, the sky is full of knives again, inky with the seep of death. I hadn't noticed until one of the twins, Maria maybe, came into the study. She grabbed me by the hand and pulled me to the window. Without a word, she nodded her head to show me the sky. I don't know how to interpret these signs; for some people, they're omens. I bit my lip. The festering breath of the assassins was already hovering over us.

The marauders don't need to break down the door, they simply come into the house. One of them, Breton Claude, grabs Félix by his pyjama collar as he's coming down the stairs and smacks him so forcefully that he crashes to the other end of the room, behind the sofa. Félix passes out, in shock. Soledad rushes at the man, and Sonia leaps at him. Like two tigresses they cling to him, biting at his hands. The man throws Soledad back against the door. He flings his free arm against Sonia's face, breaking two of her upper teeth. In the meantime the others are destroying everything with sledgehammers—in the study, in all the bedrooms, everywhere. Maria is holed up in one of the bedrooms, she is screaming and the screams alternate with the blows splintering the furniture and the doors.

They're taking us, me and Soledad.

Wrenching us along, dragging us by the hair, they haul us down the hill. The cars pull out of the bushes, and the men push us each in a car. Then we are folded into the night.

Wedged in the backseat between two sweaty thugs, I try to imagine what a woman who lets herself be seduced by these animals might look like. I strive in vain to give her a face, features. How, I ask myself, disgusted, I wonder how a woman can have a man like this by her side, in her bed—a man who comes home night after night with his hands red with his victims' blood. How can she let him touch her, let herself be stroked by those hands, accept that mouth on her, the touch of love from a mouth that orders death night after night? An executioner, a murderer close to you, against you, inside you. You hear him snoring, you feel his breath, you breathe the same air he breathes. You watch as he placidly gives himself over to sleep. It is a devil's game. Only the devil could do this.

The hour has come. The bastards will sink their fangs in my flesh and the flesh of my daughter, marking us both to the bottom of our souls.

II

GRANADA, 1974

FIFTEEN WAS AN IMPORTANT BIRTHDAY. In Granada, where I grew up, families from Argentina, Mexico, and Chile held lavish feasts and balls to introduce their fifteen-year-old daughters to society. Soledad had been hospitalized for depression again, so I spent my birthday with María Luz. Which was nothing new: I couldn't imagine my life without María Luz.

I remember our conversation that day. María Luz, who had her own weight of memory to bear, had chosen my fifteenth birthday to introduce me to myself. We had just finished lunch, relaxed. But I could sense a kind of restlessness in her, she was preoccupied, fiddling with bread crumbs, sliding them around on the tablecloth. It got me worried, too. How was Soledad, I asked; they had spent the morning together.

When María Luz began to speak, her voice reverberated in my head, deafening.

"I hesitated about telling you this for a long time, Junon."

She couldn't control the quavering, and it was a huge effort for her just to pull together the fragments of her story.

"I've put it off," she went on, "I've been putting off the day when I would have to do this."

What armour did I have? I started shaking too. *Here we are*, I thought. This would be the moment the actors walked out onto the stage, into the light.

María Luz's words buzzed inside me. I was on the verge of fainting, a weight on my chest. It took all the strength I could muster to listen. She had no idea the turmoil her words were causing.

"The first time Soledad and I met was at Carmen de los Mártires. She was sitting on a stone bench, looking out over the valley. I thought, *oh, a woman who looks like me.* It wasn't the first time I had seen her frozen like that, always on the same bench, gazing toward the mountains or wandering around, lost on the shady footpaths. It was like she'd always been there, as if she had been born among those stones, as if she had grown there like the cypress trees. Like them, she was ravelled up in her silence. I don't know what came over me, but that day I decided to sit next to her. The spring had been warmer than usual, and by June the heat was debilitating. It was probably the heat that made it hard for her to walk. She was very pregnant by then, and she had collapsed on the bench. She looked at me sideways. The late-afternoon air was still, and something began to thrum. It wasn't the dragonflies or the bees or the sparrows, their frenetic ballet, but Soledad's voice. She began to speak—of the splendour of the amethyst-coloured bougainvillea that rush up the walls, the doves that live peacefully in shady clefts at the base of these century-old trees. *How I envy them*, she stammered. *I envy them.* I understood instinctively that Soledad was like me, a creature in search of solace. In the gardens, under the trees, she and I were both looking for something: something fresh and new, a sign, some consolation on bad nights. Above all, something to soothe what was torn inside us. We had arrived there each with our burden of pain. I had survived Spain, a country terrified beyond anything imaginable—Spain under Franco, the blue shirts, Spain in the 1930s. The sadness that had come into my life early on—it was anchored in the depths of my being in those years—that sadness had remained. Like Soledad, I fought, and I am still fighting. Life, I've learned, is nothing more than a very long road along which you have to fight to stay upright, to move forward. On that road I found Soli, and you."

As she spoke, María Luz paid no attention to the questions I lobbed at her, like obstacles I tried to put in her way. But the story was more than just the weft of my life, more than a thread to follow. As she spoke, her words became a fount of luminous water for me. She held my hand and gave it a little squeeze. This was a language only she understood but it released me, saved me from my venom: little by little, it dissolved.

Unruffled, her voice faint as a trickle of water following its course, she went on.

"The Alhambra, and especially how peaceful it was there at the Carmen, made Soledad lighter. The lush garden was a respite from the darkness, it was a place where colours, light, and the burble of water prevailed. From morning to night, Soledad walked in that paradise of flowers, orchards, and fountains. She loved the colours, rust and ochre, red and especially the blue that adorned the walls. She would touch the stones, press her forehead to the rough tree trunks, in search of an answer. Sometimes she stayed for hours, staring at the walls, peering at the curved drawings and the mysteries of the engraved texts for a sign, something to plumb the chasm that had opened up beneath her feet on a January night. There, in the garden, Soledad wanted to be a bird. She was struggling against a clamour within her body, in her soul, and in her blood."

"The clamour was me, the child she didn't want?"

My voice broke, pitiful. I couldn't resist the need to grab every opportunity to show my wounds. María Luz's face tensed. "Junon," she countered, her eyes still closed, "life doesn't always let us choose our own troubles. But it is up to us to find a way to quiet or quell them."

She paused. She opened her eyes briefly and looked up at the sky, watching the flight of a bird soaring free.

"Soledad was never one for long speeches. All I got was what she was willing to confide. I never asked her a single question: it would have felt like I was digging into her flesh. We traded confidences, mine for hers, and down in the well of our silences we knew how to find each other.

"She had come back from a trip to her country. She'd left at nineteen to come live in Spain. She loved Spain, she said, she was madly in love with it, with all her many lives. And they took everything from her. How many times did she try to describe the vengefulness that drove Duvalier and his men? She always gave up, in the end, and broke down sobbing. *I know what they're like, that breed*, I told her to calm her down. She shook her head. *No, luz de mi alma, you don't know, you can't know.* So I told her about Guillena, the seventeen women. They were between twenty and seventy years old when they were arrested in the summer of 1937. They had relatives who were unionists or anarchists—a husband, fiancé, or brother who supported the Republicans. For two months they were tortured. The Falangists cut their hair and paraded them through Guillena. That fall, in November, they were taken to the cemetery in Gerena by Franco's men and the Civil Guard. They were shot and thrown into a pit. Among them was tía Eugenia, my mother's sister, and my aunts Alfonsina and Rebecca. Tía Rebecca was about to give birth. Another time, I travelled with Soledad to Madrid, to the Almudena cemetery. Early August. In the front of the wall where they were shot, I told Soledad about the tragic fate of another group of girls, Las Trece Rosas, as they've been called since the assassination. The thirteen roses were activists in the Unified Socialist Youth, arrested a month after the end of the war. On August 5, 1939, after a sham trial, they were shot. They were between sixteen and twenty-nine years old.

"This, Junon, is what Soledad and I were talking about, about the foundational crimes of society, crimes we're still slow to name, which we still hide. We talked about the same thing, hundreds and thousands of times, we plummeted into the furthest reaches of pain, the depths of agony, but we knew—we knew this was the price of rebirth. Drunk on our secrets, overwhelmed, we parted at twilight at the gates of the Alhambra only to meet again in our minds in the labyrinth of sleepless nights. Soledad, like me, slept with one eye open, anguish and fear making their rounds, invading her dreams and her silence. Some evenings, she was so terrified that she would come over to my house. When I woke, there she was. Such a sad look in her eyes.

"Soli, Soli," I said. "*Mis tristezas*," I whispered, borrowing the poet's verses, "*I leave them to those who made me suffer, but I have forgotten what they were and I don't know where I left them.*"

"Luz de mi alma," she replied, smiling weakly, "there was no light there anymore, not a glimmer anywhere.

"At first, she couldn't escape her silence. Most of the time, at the San Cecilio hospital, where I had to bring her so often, she was paralyzed, looking away, her hands clenched, knees pressed tight. All of a sudden she would shudder in disgust and all the horrors of the world passed before her eyes, tears streaming down her face. Since that horrible night of Sunday, January 5, the wound had grown wider. It pressed down with all its weight and each time she remembered those who ran away, all those who avoided the road to Mika's house. The wound—the sorrow—was pried open in large part because of those good people who'd walled them up inside their agony. How many people gave them nothing but a distant smile? Was everyone poisoned by mistrust and suspicion? After their crime, when the men who had tortured them abandoned your grandmother on the road to Delmas, she asked for help along the way, but she realized that she wasn't welcome, even in the homes of people she knew. She would never have thought anyone would dare turn away a woman in that state in the middle of the night. So she had to drag herself alone along the road, feeling the sore extent of the spinelessness, the ugliness of those cowards, until a man, braving the danger and the executioners' wrath, finally stopped. He was a doctor. He had spent the night at a patient's bedside and was on his way home shortly before dawn. He turned a corner and had driven barely three hundred metres when he heard a woman screaming. She was begging for an ambulance, banging on doors, but they stayed stubbornly closed. The woman who was screaming was a merchant, she'd left her house in the middle of the night to get to town early to sell vegetables. She had pulled Mika out of the ditch where she'd fallen, weak and too broken to go on into the night. That slight woman with emaciated hands had managed to lift Mika up to make her drink some water.

"The man stopped his car at the side of the deserted road. Mika only regained consciousness two weeks later, hovering between life and death in that same doctor's clinic. He cared for her with such dedication then and treated her for several years afterwards."

POISONED MEMORY

*What moon will gather up
your grief of lime and oleander?*
—Frederico García Lorca, "El paso de la siguiriya"

I WAS BORN IN SPAIN, in Granada, where Soledad went when she fled the island in March 1958. She had lived there for two years already, earlier, in university. She had wanted to become an architect. She loved flamenco, and with her throaty voice gave such life to the "Siguiriya" and the "Solea gitana," those solemn songs, sober and majestic, that churn up from the bottom of the belly and somehow manage to convey all the tragedies of the human condition.

The butchers had taken everything from her, María Luz said, leaving her only the weeping moons to gather her sorrow and her voice to lament—the voice that from time to time floated up in a corner of the house, a desperate cry as she sang "El paso de la siguiriya": "¿Adónde vas, siguiriya, con un ritmo sin cabeza?¿Qué luna recogerá tu dolor de cal y adelfa?"

María Luz claimed that I was supposed to be born in October, but Soledad had decided otherwise. She would never have allowed such an affront: she associated October with Duvalier, terror, the repressive debauchery of all the rabble celebrating his rise to power. So Soli had spent July and August walking, every single day. Sometimes she wandered for days on end, covering incredible distances, to try to bring on labour.

María Luz had never been a midwife, but Soledad didn't want anyone else with her, so she had to learn.

"The day you came out of her belly, right away you cried your first cry, then you opened your eyes. When she saw you, Soledad was speechless, astounded."

"Did she expect me to have horns and claws?"

María Luz was accustomed to these kinds of remarks, which I let slip all the time without thinking—a sign, María Luz said, of my yearning for a mother's love—a love Soledad had never been able to give me. As usual, María Luz ignored my sulking.

"I had prepared bottles of milk," she went on. "I had hired a young woman to take care of you. You wriggled gently in my arms, trying to bury your whole tiny fist in the flower of your mouth. Your small pink fist, so energetic and determined. Soledad was trembling, she couldn't take her eyes off you. I could see her frail body shivering. I left the room to set the milk to cool, and after a moment I heard a cry. I rushed back into the room with you, still clutching you, huddled against me. Soledad was squalling her pain. She vomited her hatred in a shuddering swell of sobs, but her face was dry. For the first time, I felt the real weight of so much suffering. You looked so patient bundled in my arms. You had already gotten used to sorrow in her womb. You were waiting quietly with your fist in your mouth. Suddenly Soledad took out her breast, and without a word, I laid you in her arms."

◆

My childhood was wild and solitary. Soli was absent, even in the way she looked at me—she was raw, and it pushed me away, to nothingness, to wandering. I was so alone in my silent despair. What could I have asked of her? How could I ask for what she couldn't give? What hope was there for either of us? I begged for her impossible love with all my might, spinning alone in the blind nights. I was looking for something to hang on to. María Luz fought to block out that sadness, to protect me with her imperfect words. Soli, reclusive in her silence, was always a little bewildered at the sight of me. Soli, who only ever paid silent attention to me—silence punctuated by withering sighs that burst from her chest. And there was María Luz, trying to fill the void. Luckily there was Mika, too, my grandmother, whose self-sacrifice and gentleness never ceased to amaze me. She never went a single month without writing to us, and she made a point of coming to stay for a few weeks every year. Without her, without her presence, and of course without María Luz, I would have spent my whole childhood like a bird screaming alone on its branch, as the song goes.

Soledad had made silence an absolute rule, an inviolable fortress, and anytime she felt threatened, she berated me, hysterical: no words, no talking. In those moments, an intense pain heaved through my body. My blood ran cold.

The day I turned sixteen, María Luz, beaming, asked Soledad to put her arm around me for a photo. Soledad frowned. She had spent the afternoon cooking and humming, singing her usual blues. Without a word, she opened the door, leaped over the railing, and started to run. María Luz panicked and followed. She ran after her for a few minutes, trying to catch up, but she had to give up. Soledad didn't come back until long after midnight. Forgive me, she said. I had never dared to tell her how painful her silence was for me. I could hardly believe that the woman who had given birth to me had once been a cheerful girl, happy to be alive—once, before all the horror.

Soli's future, María Luz repeated, had disappeared, it was annihilated that night. Sunday, January 5, 1958. But all the hatred that Soledad spewed out, I absorbed. I sipped it, I drank it down, and as the years went by I became consumed with a desire for revenge that was as overwhelming as my longing for love.

By the time I turned seventeen, still an orphan of the world as well as by birth, I was spitting fire. I went around with fury in my belly, aimlessly, searching for my soul. The silence droned on without respite. Although we lived together, I had forgotten what Soli's voice sounded like.

Only María Luz was watching, her shadow always over me.

María Luz taught me joy, she taught me to love the wind, the rain, the smell of the earth, to name the stars and talk to the birds. She loved her country, and the woman who caught me, who caught my first smile, was able to replace the acrimony flowing through my veins. "I christened you as a daughter of this land, which no hatred, strong as it may be, can strip of its wonders. The rust and ochre of Al-Andalus will dwell within you, along with my love and Soli's. She does love you, our Soli," she said, leaning her forehead against mine. I pouted, but María Luz went on. "In her own way, of course, she loves you. And you know it." She changed the subject: "To love Spain, to love any land, you have to know its history."

María Luz gave me books to read, and she brought me along when she travelled, on holiday, all over the country. I walked through the streets of Andalusia to the foot of the sierra. I learned to name the stones laid by the Phoenicians, Carthaginians, Romans. I learned to decipher Spain. Yet all the gardens of Andalusia, all the love that María Luz had for me—none of it could lighten the weight that rested on my shoulders. It poisoned my blood, and it had made my life a road paved with delusions. What I was looking for didn't exist in Spain. It was something neither Soledad nor María Luz could give me.

WHAT LIFE REMAINS

THE YEAR I TURNED EIGHTEEN, Mika visited us again, as she did every year, since Soledad would never again set foot on the island of her birth. That year, Mika decided to stay longer; I was thrilled. Spring came early, rainy and grey, but my heart was full of a light and softness I'd never known—all those precious, sweet hours, though now without tears, that I got to spend with my grandmother. Every time she came to visit, my grandmother tried to reach out to me. She was desperately casting about for some way to talk about what had happened, but the story kept slipping away. Just as I'd waited patiently at birth for Soledad's breast, I waited for my grandmother to come to me, to leave the world of silence, a world she had lived in for so long—not the silence imposed by the men who'd tortured her, but a stillness she had reached of her own free will, with *Two wings, a violin, and so many countless things, things unnamed.* So the poet wrote.

That day, we were in Guadix. María Luz wanted to take advantage of what remained of the day: the birdcalls and commotion, the last breath of sunshine in the valley, the bliss and laughter of lovers. She wanted to dawdle, to stroll through the narrow streets. Mika and I went back to the cavern of the hotel room. Mika flopped onto her bed, but she was agitated, she couldn't sit still. After a moment she got up and walked to the garden, and I followed. I'd noticed that the closeness, the intimacy between us during these trips had a peculiar effect, a kind of mutual expectation that grew chafed and feverish. Every moment was a prelude to a confession, or rather a revelation, a long time coming. And each time I implored a god who was deaf to my prayers that Mika would at last come to me, that she might tell me herself what had happened in January 1958.

María Luz got back late. "She must have forgotten herself in a bodega," Mika said, "in conversation with a bottomless glass of wine." Was she hoping that María Luz's return would save her? But I followed her, and soon we were both gazing at the sunset, the city in the background, our hearts in our mouths. In the startling sweetness of twilight, she began to speak.

"There is no one else in the world who can tell you what I'm about to tell you, Junon. And you'll never know what it's taken for me to be able to bring it up. I feel…"—she paused briefly and sighed—"I feel as if what remains of my life is going to drain out in my words. Believe me, nothing I've lived since that fateful night has been as painful." She drew herself up, as if jolted by a bolt of courage. "There are things you need to know that only I can tell you, and it is up to me to provide you with this information even if it means dragging us both down…My child, you have to know."

Mika was still reluctant to edge closer to what she'd tried to hold at bay for so long, but in that moment she was moved by something stronger than even her will. She finally gave in, diving into the pit of memory, and exhumed everything that was still within reach. I couldn't imagine where her composure came from, the astonishing serenity of this woman in her seventies. She hated when people latched on to the hearts of others to unload their grievances.

"Those who are hungry for attention suffer too much. So my serenity comes from silence. Lamenting your fate isn't always a sign of humanity, you know?"

She looked at me intensely, as if she could read my mind.

"It's always risky," she declared, a note of concern in her voice, "to set yourself up as a judge. The word justice, which they say has two sides, is like the word freedom: it can only reach us from the bottom of a cacophony, a muddle of ideas we wish were clever, and through which we wade blindly."

As she spoke, my grandmother rubbed her hands together as if brushing off some stubborn dust or debris. Looking at her, it occurred to me that there was immeasurable suffering in her words and in that gesture, though she managed to put it aside to try to reach me, and that effort represented greater suffering still. I looked at her helplessly.

"First of all," she added, "I would like you to understand what it means to choose silence. I have never claimed to be the keeper of truth. But by coming up against impostors and their tricks, I was looking for my own truth. That night they chose to destroy it, stabbing their fangs into me, and Soledad. That is their truth. That disgrace is theirs."

"They'll have to face it, abuelita. Sooner or later, I know it, they'll have to face those truths, own up to what is theirs. Otherwise—" my voice broke, "we're just abetting their dominance, how impervious they are. It's unforgivable."

María Luz came in, and put an end to our conversation that evening. But later I insisted, I wanted Mika to tell me how she had felt that night, the night of every evil, when they left her, half-dead, on that deserted road.

STITCHES OF MEMORY

"**DUVALIER HAD MADE SURE HE WAS THERE** while his men were torturing me—it was malevolent, a taste for the obscene. He was there all night. His face was impassive, he never flinched as he watched every strike and blow. And in his presence, his henchmen were that much more zealous, anxious to get into his good graces. How many hours did they spend beating me, slapping me? They took turns—two by two, to be more efficient. He stood, approving, his eyes half closed. Duvalier would sometimes execute prisoners himself; a few days earlier, he had shot two young men in their twenties in one of the palace dungeons.

"There were two women among my torturers—Rosalie Bosquet, known as madame Max Adolphe, and one of her lieutenants, Lysiane somebody, who went on to become a minister.

"Until the last minute Duvalier hoped I would throw myself at his feet and beg for mercy. He had only opened his mouth twice, first to tell them, furious, to break my fingers: *That'll teach her to trade in brooms and needles for a quill.* His voice grew more nasal as it filled with loathing. He was incensed that Mika Pelrin clenched her teeth, stared the assassins in the eyes, and let them carry on with their despicable task. The first one who came at me was a man named Luc Désir. Now, in my sleepless nights, I can still hear the sinister crack of my bones, the bones of my fingers, my hands, given over to those bloodthirsty bastards.

"The second time he opened his mouth, he gave the order to let me live. *She must stay alive*, he told them. *She must remain a living example. Everyone will know what François Duvalier is made of.* That was what he said. Then he got up and walked toward the door. Before he left, as if throwing dogs a bone, he turned back: *I'm leaving now. The carcass is yours if you want it; tuck in.* All of this was taking place, my girl, in the basement of the National Palace.

"After Duvalier had gone, I don't know how many of them assaulted me, I don't remember anymore. There must have been seven, maybe more. But all I could think about was Soledad. In the depths of that night of horror, I understood that I was undertaking a terrible apprenticeship. I was shucking off a dead skin, and I was leaving behind my role as a mother to become a sister in sorrow, the sister of my own beloved child. I didn't know if she was still alive. She had been handed over to hatred, to those animals. From then on, Soledad and I would travel together, sisters in the same battered body. As I dragged myself along the road where I could have died, all I could think about was her. With all my strength I held on to the hope of seeing her alive again."

Mika paused for a few moments. Was she trying to see out whether she was able to go on, to tell me what happened next? It was intense: she was staring right at me, but she couldn't see me anymore. It was night. Both of us had insomnia, and we would meet over a cup of tea and talk, often until the early hours. The sudden crack of the branches of the holly oak against the window brought Mika back to the kitchen. I knew she was coming back from far away. She shook her head, like a dog. It looked like she was talking to herself.

"How was it possible? How come the neighbours…They were so close, how come they heard nothing?" She sighed again as she thought of how many times she had agonized over the same pointless question: how was it possible that no one had intervened?

"After they left me on the road, I wasn't sure I would survive. Only a few cars went by, and it didn't even occur to me to try to stop one. I couldn't think, I couldn't stand, I didn't even have the strength to scream. After all these years, so many small details seemed unimportant, I thought they had drowned in a sea of horrors, yet they come back, insistent. So I stop, I listen to those details—what if? What if it hadn't happened that way, what if that woman hadn't chosen to help me? What if she'd been run over by a car when she leapt recklessly into the middle of the road to try flag down someone who might take pity on me?

"The woman lifted me. She was stumbling and tripping over the stones and I was covered in blood but with the little strength I had I tried to help her. Once she had laid me on the embankment, I understood just what I had left behind in that ditch: a part of my past, a part of my resistance, and so much of what I had wanted, so many of my dreams. Do you understand, Junon?" Mika went on. "It was such a strange feeling, there was such a huge absence; the whole world was suddenly missing, so many futile, frivolous things—everything around me. The only thing was pain, and it blocked out everything else. It had another face, its features even more abhorrent, if that's even possible, than the butchers'. How can I explain this to you, my child? I was long past fear, because I had witnessed every aspect of evil. Evil embodied by the diabolical power of Duvalier, that servant of Lucifer. I had been to hell."

◆

Tears streamed down my face, I was sobbing, inconsolable. Mika stood up and took me in her arms. Through my sobs she caught the word victim and broke away from me. She took a deep breath.

"Yes, I have been the victim of an abominable crime," she said firmly. "And the perpetrators of that crime have never been even the tiniest bit worried. But I've always refused to speak or behave like a victim. There's something perverse about victimhood. I'm still suffering, terribly, especially when I hear so many unacceptable things from people I never thought capable of such blasphemy. I don't condemn anyone, but neither do I deny the resentment that often rises in my throat. Some people, you can imagine, thought I was too proud. I had hanged myself with my own rope, they told themselves, I had sunk my own ship."

My grandmother was speaking more loudly now. When she heard herself, she cowered back in the chair, as if she had long since forgotten that voice, as if it was someone else's voice inside her.

"Sometimes I tell myself that my life was shipwrecked," she said very slowly, in a rustle of words. "I haven't been able to accomplish what I wanted. And sometimes I wonder if civilization itself is sinking into a sea of violence."

"What do you regret?"

"I have so many regrets," she replied sadly. "I regret so much that I didn't know how to protect my children better. Not being able to rely on my own means, giving in too much to what society expects from a woman. And not being able to be clear-headed about Charlot. Did I unconsciously accept comfortable mediocrity? I still wish I'd been able to see it sooner, to know what it was I had to escape: the madness of Charlot's success, the seven-horned beast that ate him up from the inside, and which consumed me in turn. I tried to ignore his petulance, his hunger to possess everything, what he pompously called success, and which he had ended up achieving like so many others—by closing his eyes on the abominations. When you accept a man in your life, you deny everything, you divorce yourself from the world because he becomes the world. Which is no more and no less than what he wants. Your great-aunt Clarisse used to say that."

"Tell me more about Clarisse, abuelita. That rush of life about her, her overflowing energy…It's fascinating."

My grandmother's eyes gleamed, though she hesitated. She was sleepy, and it was almost dawn. Soon we would hear Soledad's voice, her mournful song. But Mika liked to talk about Clarisse, and she forgot her fatigue.

"Clarisse was two years older than me, and when we were children, she felt she had to protect me. Even today, that hasn't changed. If anything, our mother's death made the instinct stronger. When I was young, no one dared attack me. As soon as a fight broke out around me, Clarisse would come running, like Zorro. She was the one who stood up to Papa on my behalf. She told anyone who would listen that she was willing to walk through fire for her sister."

"You were that close?"

"We were inseparable, despite our differences, and even when I lost patience with her. We're still close. She never recovered from the events that night, which almost cost me my life."

"Living with her must have been kind of intense."

"That's an understatement! Whenever she was around, we would end up having long discussions. One day, she declared barefacedly that the priests had fucked our men and made them crazy."

"She didn't mince words!"

"I made the mistake of asking her what evidence she had that these Breton, French, Canadian, and other priests, who stood at the helm of our venerable educational institutions, had been sexually abusing the boys. She shot me right down; scandals like that were common all over the world, she said. Everywhere, she ranted, abuse by the clergy was shoved under the rug, and here I was, a journalist and naive enough to believe that in this miserable country where they write the laws they might be sparing our children! We don't talk about it, and do you know why? Because from a very young age we are indoctrinated, it's a code of silence. Those who endure those traumas would never breathe a word! *You know that*, she told me. And of course among those who've lived through this abuse, some inevitably ostracize whoever is mad enough to open their mouths, to denounce it. *And don't forget*, Clarisse added, *that this abuse happens under a double submission; we know that so many of these young people end up in the seminary—the Lord's own whorehouse—because their parents can't afford to pay for their studies.*"

"How can you argue with that?"

"She wasn't wrong, but she was sharp and bullish. She charged blindly, a beast in the ring. I warned her not to generalize, but she got carried away and eventually she would wear me down. She always had to have the last word. But Clarisse had a good heart. She put others first, though she had no sense of moderation. *Clarisse is without measure in love, as in hate*, Bé would say. She always prompted as much hatred as appreciation around her."

Mika looked at the time and sighed.

"So many memories for such a small life, Junon. Why don't we have a way to erase memories, my child? Do you know how much pleasure it would give me to erase whole decades of my life?"

She was both serious and almost amused by this revelation.

"I'm sure you choose to ignore certain memories," I replied. "Those that are tucked so far back it's like they never existed."

"Ah, but you're wrong, my Junon. There are things I don't talk about, but only because I don't know where to find the words. What's sadder than silence, I keep asking myself, over and over again. But shouldn't we also resist the allure of forced or unrepentant confessions, the impulses that drive us to speak or to hear others speak, at the risk of trivializing what's most important? Do you understand what I mean?"

I knew what Mika was referring to; Soledad and I were in therapy. I'd been seeing someone for almost four years, without the relief I had expected but I kept going anyway, and maybe one day I would be able to contain the anger that lifted me up like a tide, surging, thrashed me, and took away any semblance of rest.

Mika's reactions often confused me; I had talked about it with Gilberto, my therapist. He felt Mika was still in denial, which helped protect her from pity. *It allows her to maintain her dignity and intimacy*, he explained. I thought of Gilberto's words.

"How do we decide what is important and what is not, abuelita," I asked Mika. "I've been begging you for years, every time you come here, to tell me about Charlot. Surely he's not just the buffoon you make him out to be, authoritarian, cowardly? You would never have married such a man, I know it."

She could hear the judgment in my voice. She drew a breath.

"Thinking back, I tell myself that excess can be the cause of many mistakes. I was so rebellious when I was twenty, so disgusted by the society I came from, that I chose a man I thought was the opposite of all the people around me who were bloated with what they called their origins. But I married a man who was no man at all, that's the truth."

"That's such a cliché, abuelita!"

"All of this is a bit confusing for me, as you can see, I admit, even though I've given it a lot of thought. One thing is certain: I accept my contradictions, Junon. But yes, Charles-Émile was a great disappointment. Before, I used to tell myself that I'd been duped. The man pulled one over on me! But with time I sometimes wonder if I was unfair to him, whether I asked him to make an effort that even I couldn't: to become truly, fully human. Absolute humanity. It's the little things that make you understand. How complicated it all is, my Junon." Mika looked at the time, startled. "It's almost six o'clock in the morning!" She stretched. "I have never been so tired. It's time to rest."

Her eyes were about to close, and her cheeks were warm when I kissed her. She stood up and took the book she had left on the table, *The Confessions of Saint Augustine*. With small steps, she climbed the stairs.

Mika had extended her stay with us, as if she was reluctant to leave Soledad and me. A blazing summer glinted over Andalusia every day, and María Luz, Mika and I zipped around like ants from Seville to Ronda and Zahara de la Sierra in Cádiz to take part in the processions for the feast of Corpus Christi, when entire villages took to the streets. We didn't want to miss the San Juan bonfires for anything in the world. One evening, on a beach—in Alpujarras? I don't know anymore, though the memory of that night still moves me—in a childish burst of joy, Mika was quivering as she gazed into the flames. The sparks seemed to come not from the fire but from her heart. She started clapping her hands and said that we should light fires all over the world at the same time on the same day to purify the world.

By the end of October, she was gone again. There's no way to explain what she took with her when she left. The emptiness her departure left for me was impossible to fill. Soledad was inconsolable, though she had seen little of her mother, spending most of her time alone in her studio. But that summer a miracle had happened: Soledad had decided to go back to painting, and she threw herself into it, like her aunt Clarisse. I'd never dreamed she would pick up a paintbrush again. María Luz was elated, she went around singing "España, camisa blanca"—hope, at last, for a tormented soul.

Already in the first days of summer, Soledad was reborn. Her painting was a light in the dark. She had started selling her paintings in the square. She got up at dawn, and sometimes worked until nightfall.

Soledad's paintings, Mika said, especially how she mixed colours, reminded her of Clarisse's. Soledad worked to Bessie Smith, Dinah Washington, and others whose names I no longer know. These jazzy melodies, often slow and languid, moved her. They wove their way inside her because they caught the initial movement that became an extension of her painting. It was like she had signed a pact with Billie Holiday—that voice floated out over the silence of the studio for Soledad alone. "Trouble in Mind": Not a day went by that we wouldn't suddenly hear her singing, as if it were a prayer. Whole days she'd hum the same tune. More than a song, even one that's full of promise, Soledad's voice was a call no one could answer.

Well it's trouble, oh trouble
Trouble on my worried mind
When you see me laughin'
I'm laughin' just to keep from cryin'...

BITTER TONGUES

"**HISTORY REPEATS ITSELF.** All stories can be repeated," María Luz began. "The same story can take place at different times, in different places, under different skies, with different players and different faces."

"But can't we invent other stories, better, more beautiful ones?" I asked bluntly.

"I would be the last to deny that, Junon. Life offers us the opportunity for beautiful stories, yet sometimes we don't know."

Her eyes shone with emotion as she spoke.

"I'm telling you the truth, Junon; we don't always know how to seize these opportunities, how to be inspired by them. Sometimes one story can enlighten us or allow us to understand another. How can we forget that I was the first face you set eyes on? I was the first to kiss you, on your closed fist, I first stroked your cheek. Isn't our story beautiful?"

"And I will never say otherwise. You were also the one who taught me to love the country you call Spain, a profound love."

"And in the name of that same love, Junon, I want to tell you another story, with roots in this land and in my flesh. It belongs to both of us, since we were both born on the same soil."

She stopped, searching somewhere inside herself for words that didn't exist.

"You want to talk about the Civil War and Franco, I know that," I told her, too quickly.

She stopped me right away.

"Rather, it's what one might call the story of life on the inside under Franco. This history took place inside people—I'm thinking of the individual stories, the personal dramas of those who were plunged into the night of franquismo. There are so many things we don't know, so many lies, so many crimes unpunished. The work of commemoration," María Luz told me, "has only just begun, and I hope with all my soul that it continues, that it goes on. That what the Church did during that time comes to light, among other things. Did you know that the women who were about to be murdered were paraded around the city with their heads shaved and then forced to attend Mass? And what about the thousands of children stolen at birth by the Francoists and then given to families who were friends of the regime? All those criminals had to do was tell the mother that her child had been stillborn. There was so much silence, but also so many accomplices: the hospital staff had to be in on it."

"Forgetting settles in so easily it manages to colonize our awareness. Would it be easier to forget than to remember, María Luz?"

María Luz was too emotional, and we drove on in silence for a good part of the way. Finally, between the villages of Viznar and Alfacar, near a farmhouse called Cortijo de Gazpacho, María Luz stopped the car. We left the car on the side of the road and walked down a little hill and then back up a path lined with olive trees, their greyish leaves rustling. María Luz stood there, staring out into space, dreaming.

"It would be about here," she said suddenly, "that they murdered the poet, without any kind of trial. They say he is buried at the foot of an olive tree—in other words, his resting place is everywhere in these hills, because everyone makes their own assumptions. Others claim he was killed along the road from Viznar to Alfacar. Since those who actually know what happened will never say anything, the exact circumstances of his death will always remain a mystery. The tragic story of that man lives on in me like a splinter. When I think of him I can't help but hear the boots and rifles, the pounding of soldiers' footsteps, I see his pale face in the blue night, his brown curls, I see him going toward death. I see the hills of Viznar too, and the thousands of dead they've cradled. The repression was unthinkably bloody, Junon; these hills were the scene of countless executions."

María Luz was holding me by the arm. Shivers coursed through her whole body. She spoke of the poet as if of a loved one. I was about to ask her if she had known him.

"The historian Miguel Caballero conducted an investigation over several years to track down the perpetrators. Imagine all the challenges a historian has to overcome in order to carry out his work—the cowardice of some people, the silence of others, the indifference."

"Sometimes I think about all of it…That silence, that indifference is a form of cruelty too. I'm powerless in the face of the malice that so often defines relationships. It frightens me…I keep telling myself that I was born of rape and torture. And I confess, Luz de mi alma, sometimes I feel like my whole being is full of violence. A constant bubbling: I'm nothing but one avalanche after another, rivers of lava so hot that I'm afraid of myself."

"There is violence in human beings, my Junon, that's undeniable. It does permeate society, politics, the relationships between institutions and authorities, whatever they may be, and citizens. But it is within ourselves that human beings must seek the source of that barbarism and eradicate it. Otherwise…Well, otherwise, the beast within us bares its fangs and makes the law. I had a taste of it when I was a little girl, and until the end of time I will hold the vile memory of that cursed time. Those days of such bitter tongues began for me one morning in the summer of 1937, Junon, when I was nine years old. I had to tell my father, who was already an old man—he was much older than my mother—I had to tell him that his wife and daughter, my sister Ana Catrina, who was nineteen, had been shot by Franco's jackals. My father had been denounced for having contact with Republicans, so following the logic of those in power, his wife and daughter were arrested at the factory where they worked, along with several other family members. For two days they didn't come home. On the second evening I had prepared supper, potatoes with a piece of ham and beans. My father ate nothing, just like the day before. Silence and foreboding blanketed the village. No one dared to come to our house to tell him the news. The hours passed, my father kept his eyes closed to avoid catching mine. I must have looked so terrified. That second day, as dusk began to bury the valley, we grew more and more anxious.

"Suddenly, as the evening unfurled, I heard a whistle. I was so afraid but I went outside. Hidden behind an old oak tree was Felipe, a twelve-year-old boy. Felipe was staring at the ground, and crying. Without looking at me—he didn't have the strength—he told me everything.

"I wanted to die when I had to break the news to my father. For a long time I felt like I was the executioner, that I had felled an old man already dying of rage, defeated by Franco's sadism, which took from him two women he loved and left him with a nine-year-old girl who no longer knew how to be a child. From one day to the next, my Junon, I had become a mother to my own father, a broken man who moaned day and night.

"I learned how to cope with death in the most inhuman way when my mother and sister were taken from me. I learned to deal with hatred, with how arbitrary loss can seem, with injustice and oppression—all those evils that pinned my father to the bed he never left until he left this world. He was a good man, and I know he would have wanted so much to spare me his pain. It was a suffering that humiliated him, he was ashamed to let me see what he felt was a degradation. After my mother and Ana Catrina disappeared, my father became tangled up in his grief until his lips finally closed over his pain. Even after all these years, I still can't put words on the sorrow that overwhelmed us that night. Until I met Soledad, I had been living in silence too, because of those voices inside me: my mother, my sister, and so many others who had disappeared, beloved voices, voices mingled with the whimpers of a man, my father, José Rosales Benalva, crying out in pain. As Soli and I got to know each other, I opened these pages of my life and shared my terrible secret. I found the words I'd lost. As we spoke, Soledad and I, as I told her my story and as the words unfolded to meet hers, my pain took on a slightly more human form. By confiding in Soledad, I became human again. I saw myself in her."

◆

I grew up around these two women. Some days, the silence in their guts screamed louder than the wind. I drank my first gulps of milk clutching the breast of the first, the one I call my blood mother, who was wracked by sobs without ever shedding a single tear. My second mother—my mother of joy—handed me the strands of a story, and they both wove them together during those long evenings when they sat up watching for ghosts and shadows. I understood early on that a swarm of black birds flapped furiously in their souls and in their memories. There came a time when I knew I had to conquer the night so that I could at last be born.

Throughout my teenage years, my quest was strange. I often dreamed about Mika. She would be standing on top of a mountain and holding out her arms to me. I would look up along the winding path, heaped with big black stones, and, standing at the bottom, my heart beating hard, I would wonder how I could get up there.

The year I turned twenty-two, I decided to leave Soledad. I moved away without being afraid of losing her, since our shared history would go on forever. We were twinned. I moved into a small apartment on San Gregorio, in the home of a woman who introduced herself as Inés de la Cruz. She befriended me right away. I realized later that I had chosen the dimly lit, old-fashioned apartment because of doña Inés, who despite her years had an insolent elegance, and for her wonderful garden. The garden was much more than a garden to her, she explained, it was a love story, written by a man who had spent five years courting her. They married and then he died suddenly the day after their wedding. I couldn't help laughing, because doña Inés herself had started to laugh, an unnatural, harsh laugh, like neighing.

"¡Pura verdad, hija! I laugh about it now, but for a long time I cried. Though I've always had company…"

Gracefully, she gathered the corners of her silk shawl and pointed to the bushes that lined the garden.

"There," she said to me, "do you hear them? Songbirds nest here. They're so noisy at the end of the afternoon, constantly bickering. Not to mention doves, turtledoves, finches. I'm never alone."

The air was growing pleasantly crisp and thick with the smell of flowers; I recognized the incomparable scent of jasmine and orange blossoms. I adopted Inés's garden, though I still went to Soledad's house in the evenings, and sometimes slept there.

Soledad was going through a phase when painting allowed her to vomit up the previous day's wreckage. With each seething stroke she stabbed her brush at the canvas, which all too often ended up torn or scorched. Yet you could tell: in spite of everything, she had found a way that would, in time and in different forms, lead toward the serenity she longed for. Alongside her hard charcoal lines, there were oils, silhouettes of women with soothing curves, but also a clutter of canvases with dark shapes—women too, dismembered, hanged, sheared, fragmented, crumpled women draped in veils of sadness and mourning, which she usually painted in the middle of the night.

We could see her coming and going, possessed by these images as if they were spirits. One of the paintings, entitled *Procesión*, she'd made with photos inlaid against a background of ochre and sand. Mika was there, from various times in her life, and Bé, Toni; María Luz, her sister Ana Catrina and their mother doña Angela; and Clarisse, Hortense, Jeanne, Sonia, Maria, and I marched along, single file, along a steep road on the edge of a cliff. Another painting, *Hermanas*, was a delirious collage on a red background, where

Soledad painted Clarisse with half of Jeanne's face, and Jeanne with half of Mika's, and then Mika and I, joined at the navel. And so on. My nights at the time were an incoherent sequence of film run backwards—always the same, the tragic stories of Mika and Soli, which poured into me relentlessly. They crashed into me like stones dropping into a well, mingling in my dreams with the macabre creatures Soli invented. Apocalyptic visions hounded me through restless nights.

I was stumbling through the beginning of film school. I was convinced that only testifying could give my life meaning. I had to see for myself, and to make people understand life under dictatorships. I didn't want to invent lives, just to present them as they were. How could I speak the unspeakable? How could I find the words? Despite my distress, I didn't want to give in to the temptation of leaving the trace of my fingers on a parchment of woe. I needed to scream, to rip off the mask, the stubborn refusal of a scrambled memory. It was too sterile. I was only able to get free the day I started picking up the stitches again and tacking all the ends back together. It was during one of those nights, on January 5, that I decided to force dawn to break. I understood then that I had to go back to the source of unremitting death. How far back? To the original wound, the very first assault, the first lie? Backwards through the bloodshed, each slash, deliberate and deadly.

FORCING THE DAWN

"IT SEEMS THAT PEOPLE in your grandmother Mika's country have reached the limit of what they're willing to put up with." That's how Soledad tells me that the country of her birth is caught up in political upheaval, which eventually leads to the departure of the sea pig who's been running the show. I remember coming across a picture of him, Baby Dòk, and he looked remarkably similar to a *scotoplanes globose*, the kind of sea cucumber we call sea pig. This species of invertebrates lives in abysses, burying itself at the bottom of the ocean and eating whatever it digs up in the mud. Soledad's scathing pronouncement is disconcerting, and I think back to that picture, the sea pig stuffed full of everything it has come across. The country must have been just a huge swamp to him, a natural habitat he'd been splashing around in since he was born. Jean-Claude Duvalier refused to leave office, balking at calls for his resignation. In February 1986, blood is flowing again across the island. As far as the makout are concerned, Haiti is their personal trough, and there is no way they will ever let go. Once again, they set the death machine in motion, and the massacres come, swift and merciless. They shoot at schoolchildren, killing dozens. History doesn't repeat itself, it just marches on.

On Friday, February seventh, 1986, finally, after bleeding the island dry for fifteen years, the son of the despot François Duvalier, who inherited the presidency from his father at the age of nineteen, is forced by popular pressure to pack his bags. It's on the radio, on TV around the world. I can't sit still.

I've never set foot in Haiti. Soledad explains with uncharacteristic indifference that a society defined by social exclusion is upheld by crime and favouritism. Did Baby Dòk's departure challenge the logic of that system? Soli doubts it. Privilege will remain the law of the land, she thinks. "I don't want to talk about it anymore! Understand?"

Her tone brooks no reply. I can sense the rage quivering inside her.

That night I must have been screaming in my sleep. When I open my eyes, Soledad is in my room. "You're having nightmares again," she says flatly before closing the door.

Half-awake and shaken, I wonder whether I should go make myself a cup of lavender tea to calm down or flip through my photos. I need to see my mother's faces: what confirmation, what other mystery might I discover? The herbal tea can wait. I have a bunch of photos of Soledad. I carry my camera with me all the time and follow her around, taking pictures of her even when she is sleeping. Often she brushes me away; *there's not a day goes by without someone trying to pin me down*, she says.

I spread out the photos and move them around, mimicking her expression, tracing her half-smiles. I run my fingertips around the contours of the eyes, the lips, as if searching for truth, for a sign. Probably I am hoping to discover a crack through which I could slip in to reclaim what was stolen from me.

It isn't quite daylight yet, but I walk around the house looking for Soledad. I need to talk to her. She must be in her studio…Yes, she spent the night there. "I'm burning up, I'm feverish," I tell her. "Let's go out for a walk." A soft light hovers in the skimming glow of dawn. We've barely gone a block when I turn to her abruptly.

"I refuse to live like Mika, like a snail coiled up in my shell."

"It's up to you to live differently," she replies, her voice empty.

I wonder if she knows how haunted I am by what happened in January 1958. I refuse to let that night be forgotten.

"What was stolen from you and Mika has to be returned. I'm going—I'm leaving Thursday. And nothing can stop me!"

"You should be suspicious of projects dreamed up in the heat of the moment; you said it yourself, you're burning up. You can want to do whatever you can, you can be stubborn, try to mend what's broken, only to realize after all that effort that it wasn't worth it. On the day when the moron who's just been toppled took his oath of office, I lost faith forever in the justice of men. There was always a little flame burning within me, like those little lamps that the women over there light in front of icons to pray for favours. A tiny flame at the end of a cotton wick that's tied to a piece of cork and placed in a dish in a mixture of oil and water. The lantern burns for a few days, I imagine, until the favour is granted. How long did my lantern burn for? I don't know...But I had hoped that crime couldn't go unpunished. Today Papa Tyrant rests, and Junior's just landed on holiday in the south of France—the land of human rights! Did my lamp go out on its own or did I snuff out the flame?"

As always, our steps bring us to the gardens at the Carmen de los Mártires. We sit on a bench and Soledad caresses the stone. The gesture appeases her. The minutes pass; we say nothing more. The freshness of the early morning can do nothing to soothe her pain, and for the very first time I take her in my arms. In a silent embrace, our limbs relax, and our tears run together.

◆

I search the pocket of my suitcase, looking for the address—the only one I have—but come up empty. It's as if the card vanished into thin air. Not a good time. The official at the counter looks tense. Visibly annoyed, his elbows propped on the desk, he stares at me rudely. "I have family here," I tell him again.

Prim and uptight in his uniform, the man asks me for the address again as he flips indolently through my passport. He looks around as if there might be someone else, a supervisor maybe, but everyone nearby is too busy or isn't paying any attention to his drama. Just another zealot wanting to play at being important. The airport lobby is crowded with people coming and going, dragging heavy bags. Behind the glass, all the employees look drained by the early afternoon heat.

"Since you're not willing to say where you're going..." He stops in the middle of his speech, hesitates, then shuffles away from the desk, moves his chair back, stands up. He opens the cubicle door, looks me up and down, and pulls the door closed. What's his inspection all about? Sweat drips down my spine, the heat making me uncomfortable. What was I thinking, dressed like this? A hairpin slips and a strand of my sweaty hair falls loose. I slide the pin back into place. All at once I remember that I put the address in the camera pocket. I start fumbling again, but then—stroke of genius—I change my mind. The man starts speaking to me in English and, perhaps because of the distance the language imposes between us, the tension drops. "I just can't find it," I hear myself say. I explain that I was born in Spain and grew up there, that this is my first visit to the island, maybe someone will come pick me up. Irritated, he scribbles something, stamps my passport, and hands it back to me.

◆

I've been meandering around Mika's house since I got here—Mika's room, the twins' room, which has been empty for years since they left to go live abroad, one in Mexico and the other in Venezuela. And at the end of the hallway, Soli's room. I spend long hours in this territory that is no longer my mother's, looking at the objects on the shelves: postcards, books with yellowed pages, photos of friends now forgotten. I sit on the steps of the staircase with my knees tucked under my chin, caressing the mahogany railing. If wood could talk.

During one of her outbursts, Soledad told me that when they were kids they used to race wildly along this long hallway to see who would get to the railing first and get to slide down the varnished mahogany horse, whooping. That past isn't mine yet it's so clearly imprinted in my soul, it's there, before my eyes, it's real. All these years...Time is still the same. Soldiers parading along in large covered trucks, chasing hungry youths who run around looting and settling scores. The town is on fire, there are roadblocks everywhere, tires burning. The sea pig has been gone for more than a week but resentment here smoulders on unabated. Unleashed. The smell of blood, dust, and alcohol, and the sting of tar is everywhere and grabs me by the throat. Houses are ransacked by gangs from the slums, all those neighbourhoods that landowners spit on while thieves take advantage of the pandemonium to grab whatever they can get their hands on.

With my camera slung over my shoulder and my sunglasses hiding my face, I walk around the city with a press badge I got during an internship. I never finished film school, but who cares? All I've ever done is ask myself why. Why? How? Difficult questions, asked of women who are too often mute, bereft in their distress. Questions that mostly go unanswered, though many of the answers came loud and clear during Soledad's episodes.

For example, when I was young I never imagined that I needed a father, I never tried to understand why I didn't have one, and now I wonder if something bigger than I am, some force stronger even than instinct, was telling me that the subject was forbidden, that I shouldn't talk about it. As a teenager, I would have liked to know, but I also knew I had to protect Soledad.

Curiously, in this city saturated with rage and dismay, I'm in no particular danger, nobody pays any attention to me. There are clashes, violence permeates the air and clings to the leprous walls of the cité, to the barbed wire that coddles the more opulent homes. The city is hectic and the sun, searing already in the still-new day, flashes its claws. And the dogs, everywhere, so many stray dogs, hungry and hassled.

In the neighbourhood where Mika lives, a group of teens who hang out under a gazebo at the bottom of the hill have adopted me. They all want to talk, they want to make a documentary to tell the whole world what nobody wants to hear: the weary but still hopeful voice of a population that has been scorned for too long.

"They want everything to change and to stay the same: nothing for us, everything for them, with repression as a perk!" Gabriel is tall and slender, and his body seems to pour along, long and serpentine, walking on air. His pants are held up by a rope. He lives at the bottom of the hill in one of the basins, the slums, he tells me. His eyes are red: he proudly announces that he hasn't slept since the night of February sixth. "We have decreed that we will keep vigil until the country has been completely cleaned up!" He warns me: "They won't let go, so watch your step. They hate journalists, photographers—real ones. Have you heard of Manuel Buendia? He was a journalist who wrote a book about what the CIA did in Mexico. He was shot right in the middle of Mexico City two years ago. I dream of being a journalist too. But here we only have our dreams."

"You have your dignity."

Gabriel's reply is blunt, his words clattering like stones.

"Honestly, I'm sick of hearing that word tossed around over and over again. They bring up dignity at the drop of a hat, as if it's supposed to be any consolation. A very poor one, believe me: don't you know how scarce dignity is in this country? Journalists and politicians are sold, and cheap. They get offered trips, conferences, bank accounts. Same for a lot of NGOs—many of them are supposed to deliver aid, but they're nothing more than CIA gravy trains. How many are filling their pockets from state coffers? They're just working for death agencies. Where is the dignity? Mine, my dignity, is to lie prone in my bed at night clutching my stomach, my mouth clamped shut as hunger screams in my belly.

"I'm eighteen," Gabriel goes on, "and I've already buried my father and mother, dead before their time, dead of starvation and misery, and God only knows what they worked for. Have you seen the porters, Junon? Those men in the market with wheelbarrows loaded up like trucks, even an ox couldn't pull one alone. My father did that all his life. And it pains me—an ache, right here in my chest—how often he worked on an empty stomach. Even worse, there are men who haul dumpsters around and they still have to sell their own blood just to feed their children. It's not a metaphor, I'm serious. There's a clinic across from the hospital—they say it belonged to a man named Kambronne, a renowned vampire, a scavenger for Papa Despot for years—people could go sell a litre of blood for five dollars. That's the kind of democracy they want to build. Everyone knows that those who have just seized power, I mean the general and his cronies, are from the same school, trained by the Americans in Panama. They got their diplomas as torturers there. But they won't get us! Grenadiers—attack!"

Gabriel's words ring with faith and bitterness, a harsh cocktail, and once again I try to establish a hierarchy of suffering, only to realize immediately that there is only one single foul wound oozing everywhere.

Someone waves to Gabriel, who suddenly moves away from the group. The newcomer looks older. He strides over, distraught. "It's Jérémie!" Gabriel's voice drops, and he almost runs over to the man. They speak for a moment, gesturing. After a few minutes, Gabriel returns, crestfallen.

"Last night," he says, "the army ambushed a small group who were about to break into a lawyer's house. The lawyer was negotiating to sell orphaned children to foreigners. They crushed them...It was Jacques's crew, from La Plaine," he explains. "They were completely decimated! We tell them and tell them that we have to be more careful, that it's too easy to get in, but they just take anyone. They had gotten it into their heads to drag this lawyer to the square, to judge him. But they have no experience," he laments. "There was one kid, Jamal, not even fifteen. I warned them not to be so impulsive. The army had men everywhere. How did they know?" Gabriel looks around at his friends. They are all unarmed.

"That's for you to find out," he grumbles. "There were five of them, all of them shot!"

He clenches his fists.

"Did you hear me? They shot them all! Sometimes I wonder if we're used to it, dying like that, like cockroaches. We got used to the idea of our own death. The dirty bourgeoisie will be well pleased," he spits. "They will dance with joy. Junon, do you know what they call the street children you see everywhere? They call them kokorat, little cockroaches. They're so scared of losing their position that they want to exterminate all of us."

Gabriel looks disgusted. He is sweating profusely and wipes his face with his shirt. His ribs jut out through the bruised, purpled skin of his chest. The little group gradually disperses, unravelling like a sweater, the stitches falling away one by one. I see them moving away, the boys turning in on themselves, stumbling. Two of them, unable to stand up on their own two legs, crouch, head in their hands. Their eyes are empty, they're dizzy, high on despair and humiliation. They gravitate around Gabriel with their heads down, all of them are looking for a glimmer of hope down in the dust, in the pebbles they mindlessly kick around off the tips of their busted shoes.

Time stretches out, and no one opens his mouth. A military tune blasts suddenly from the road, crackled out at full volume over a loudspeaker. I think of María Luz. Snippets of one of our long conversations come back to me, about Franco. *Fascism exists only to dispossess you*, she told me over and over, as if I had to be convinced. Her usually melodious voice was shaking. *It takes everything from you, it never takes enough from you, it takes your very soul, do you see?* Her voice was husky as she quoted one of those great authors—Mauriac, I think, who wrote that fascism is above all the art of neutralizing the masses, of making them harmless.

The music shuts off abruptly. There isn't a sound, nothing but the dry tumble of the pebbles the boys were chucking around in the dust all around Gabriel. I feel like the world has stopped. Days, hours…Everything is caught in this strange moment, at once empty and full of something that's taking such a long time—some event, a catastrophe, or even a miracle. And why not? Because life can't be reduced to so much sorrow. As I watch them, my thoughts crash into me, they knock around inside me like a door banging. I am sinking into an unfathomable sadness. Is this harmless? I guess, up to a point: with their foolish dreams of reversing the course of things, the boys have lost their way and all they have left is mad desire buried in their entrails. They're like animals ready to pounce. Harmless, toothless, they only vaguely suspect that their destiny, which has laid out for them, drips with death, death that never strikes at random. Held up by the apparatus of repression, death will trap them, vengeful. It chooses them, marks them with its seal.

"Junon?"

The intensity in Gabriel's voice startles me. His eyes are red though he hasn't cried. He's burning on the inside, he has been nothing but a torch for a long time, an inferno that will only be put out when the explosion everyone is waiting for finally comes.

"There are men who have propped up Duvalier to the end, even after being humiliated in every possible way. How can you explain that? It's insane, it's completely insane."

"As my grandmother says, they are beasts of the deep. And this inexplicable behaviour, as you know, is nothing but the lure of power. Power is hard to resist, Gabriel. Don't be surprised if you start hearing comments, including from people you would never have thought capable of such an aberration, scrabble up to the ramparts, taking over the airwaves to defend the scum that you drove out of the country."

"That's all they've been doing since the movement started!" Willy is Gabriel's cousin. His shirt is threadbare, and he keeps his eyes on the ground, without the look of the conqueror that Gabriel has about him. "They're calling for order and for sanctions against the troublemakers that we are."

"They will eventually get what's coming to them!" Gabriel thunders. Willy is distressed.

The pain of seeing his friends shot down like pigeons is making Gabriel delirious. He's afraid too, no doubt. Look at them all: the same blood flows in my veins. Just like them, I am a child of violence.

CHILDREN OF VIOLENCE

THE NEXT AFTERNOON, in her study, in front of the window, Mika recounts with great emotion the long nights of the siege during which she was stuck against the big cabinet while the death vans hummed at the bottom of the hill.

"All night, I struggled not to sleep. No one will ever know how eagerly I longed for the grey light of dawn," she sighs.

Beneath the window, the narrow path to Toni's house is overgrown with brambles.

"Toni died a few months before Bé," Mika whispers, "almost as if they had planned it. Obviously, even to her death she never had any news of her boy. Everything she went through, the astounding sums of money paid here and there, all the promises, but nothing. Like so many others, his bones must be bleached and sifted into the dust of the burial ground in Titanyen. A secret cemetery, but everyone knows. When Toni died, Clara, her daughter, sold the house, and eventually she moved to the United States. It was such a pretty little house," Mika says sadly. "Toni had planted bamboo all around it. When there was a breeze, the leaves whistled such soothing music." She sighs heavily. "How could I forget?"

"Can we forget? I ask.

◆

Toward the end of the afternoon, I run into Gabriel on the road. We leave the spot his crew were occupying yesterday and climb up to a huge rock at the top of a steep slope. Gabriel drags me along after him, holding on to my wrist.

"May I remind you," I tell him, "that I am strong. I spent my summers in children's camps, in the Spanish countryside and in the woods."

"I don't doubt your abilities, Junon, but we're in a rush," he replies. "The sun's starting to set, and it's quick, it slips and melts into the sea without warning. It won't be long before the hill is draped in darkness. And the others must already be there, waiting for me."

It's like I'm entering the heart of the mountain. The air is steeped in blue, and the trees too. The majesty of the place takes my breath away.

"How beautiful this country is!" I can't help whispering.

"Another paradox we'll never quite understand. Nature is beautiful here and resistant and generous. Probably that's what helps us resist too. But there's such contempt for nature, too—the country is stripped by erosion, they keep cutting down trees. Duvalier wanted to cut down the trees and raze the forests to prevent rebels from hiding there."

In the crevice of a rock, I spot a clump of greenery and flowers! They're perfect, they look like orchids. I slow down but Gabriel refuses to stop for details, he urges me along. Looking up at the clouds, he wonders aloud if it's going to rain.

"The youth in the neighbourhood have set up a brigade. They're hunting the hunters. The soldiers are out patrolling constantly, and they've swapped DKWs for tanks donated by the CIA. The weeks ahead are going to be crucial," he warns me, restless. "We've formed several units, and we're planning strikes all over the nation! First we will judge the bastards and execute them, then blow up their houses. If you want to film," he says, "you'll have to wait for one of us to come with you."

Gabriel is speaking but I'm listening to his words as if they were far away. His voice resounds like a rumble, a thunderous roar emanating from a blaze where his soul burns as it awaits more bloodshed and more carnage. Here we are, I say to myself, all of us, prisoners on this island, trapped between conflict and reprisal, in a frenzy that nothing can temper.

Sensing that my mind is wandering, Gabriel calls out to me.

"If you want you could film some of our trials." I won't be seeing him for a few days, he tells me.

Suddenly he steps away from me. A few scruffy boys come forward, just like him, skinny, their faces gaunt. They hug hard in greeting, clapping each other on the back. They negotiate. After a while, the others disperse, and Gabriel comes back toward me. He takes me by the hand to guide my steps and help me avoid stepping in the ruts, while he continues to climb like a goat on a hill. When we reach the top, he turns to me. "Open your eyes wide and tell me what you see."

I don't really understand what he expects from me. Anxious, I walk around looking at him, I concentrate. Gabriel leans against a tree trunk and lights a cigarette. I can hear him breathing deeply, hungrily taking in the smell of the place. I look around and take a few steps back to join him under the tree. His lips are parched and cracked, his hands trembling. He must be withering with impotent fury. In the half-light of the waning day, I can see huge buildings perched high up in the hills. Some of them sparkle white, surrounded by barbed wire and terrace walls as high as the houses themselves. Shards of bottles spiked into the walls flicker like fireflies in the last rays of the sun.

"At the bottom, I see the basins, like holes carved out of the mountain, gullies that fill with water. And in the basins, little boxes—thousands of little boxes stacked one on top of the other, and people who look like ants from afar, and between the rows of boxes, trenches filled with trash."

Gabriel grinds out his cigarette into the ground.

"You're seeing the second country, the country beyond. Those little boxes are our homes. Those who live there are denied bread and water, a towel soaked with fresh water to quench their thirst, and school and knowledge. Those are the homes of the people who have no choice but to sell their blood, to sell their children or watch them die." As he goes on like this, I begin to tremble. He grabs my arm, roughly, with a desperate strength, as if he wants to convince me of how righteous his struggle is.

"What you see there, below, Junon," he says, his mouth hard, "is the land of those who are asked to crawl on their knees. That is what we are fighting for."

"They're going to end up shooting you. Your movement is a spontaneous uprising, and spontaneity and willpower are not enough. You need a strong organization."

"Our organization has many flaws," he replies drily, "but we have faith, don't worry! Faith we've had since we were born!"

The evening wraps around us suddenly and completely, as Gabriel said it would. The heat remains and the air is heavy, but a shiver runs along my spine, panic wending its way inside me. I am afraid for Gabriel and all the others with him. Their lives hang by a thread. Gabriel is still only a child, yet I worry that the time he has left to live is very short.

"There are so many ways to die," he says as if he were reading my mind, "but our death, here on this earth, where we are, is programmed by the merchants of death. We may as well pick our moment ourselves. We can't possibly expect to see them behind bars, so we have to take matters into our own hands. This morning, on the radio, they were going on about the unrest, street kids plundering the homes of honest people. Can you imagine the nerve? They have never lifted a finger to demand justice against all the criminals who should be rotting in prison instead of being welcomed in France or in Santo Domingo. We are going to show them what street kids can do. I swear to you, Junon, my friends and I are ready to give our lives."

Machine gun fire rattles in the distance. "The night will be noisy and hot," Gabriel announces. "Let's go home."

We turn back without speaking, stopping to check in on Mélanie, his aunt. She managed to raise five children alone and to take care of Gabriel. She runs a little restaurant at the bottom of the hill, a small place, without table or chairs, and marked by a wooden sign nailed to the beam of the awning over the shop. People—men, mostly—crouch in one corner, quietly eating their rice, fried pork and oily fritters. Since I've been here I sometimes stop to see her at work, to talk to her. Tonight, she tells me that she hasn't been able to work the last two days because of what's going on.

"The smoke from the burning tires is choking us. And there's especially the shooting, which is enough to make you lose your mind. So many people have already been injured around here," she laments. "I get up at four in the morning to go down for produce, I come back to have lunch ready by noon and then the fried foods for the evening. These days it's impossible to go into town, so I have to buy what I need here and there. I'm losing so much money. Everything is too expensive around here. But how can I not work? With all the troubles, my evenings aren't very profitable. People don't go out anymore. There are too many werewolves prowling the streets at this hour. They'll shoot you, point blank."

Mélanie is afraid for her two boys, who are seventeen and nineteen.

"It's a nasty time," she whispers sadly. "All they talk about is chasing down the werewolves, settling the score. All my life I prayed with my heart that my boys wouldn't be out on the streets. I did everything I could to avoid this. I kept them in school until the end of secondary, but after that I couldn't do it anymore. It's too expensive. And they were good students too, so smart. You see them, there? If I could afford it, they could do anything, any profession."

The fat shrieks in Mélanie's big pot, and for a second she's hypnotized, staring at the bubbles popping as if she was reading a message there. She's so proud of earning a living, and yet— "When I look at my life," she says, "life here for Black Haitians today, we are no more and no less than the illegitimate children of God, foundlings in a brothel by the sea. We are fatherless, sanpapas."

I must look bewildered, because she takes a look at my face and bursts out laughing, a big, hearty laugh that makes her sway. She wipes a tear from the edge of her eyelid with the hem of her skirt.

"What else is there to say, my dear? Can't you see that we are orphans? If we had a father who cared for us, we wouldn't be in this state, don't you think? That's what you should write in your newspaper, or what you should say in your film. Are you hearing me, my dear?"

And she turns back to her stove. I leave Gabriel and go home to Mika.

◆

Gabriel, brimming with emphatic fervour. Mélanie's impotent despair, trembling for her sons. So many young people murdered since the beginning of the revolt. The slaughter is shocking, not to mention the impunity. Yesterday's plantation slaves are yoked today in these prison democracies.

NIGHT-BLOOMING CEREUS

BACK HOME, MIKA HAS TUNED OUT, listening intently to her inner voice. She's become reclusive; she hardly goes out anymore and spends her afternoons talking about the past with Banuteau, whom she calls her old friend. I don't see her much, I'm too busy trying to learn about this country.

This afternoon, she tells me, there was heavy fire from all sides.

"I know. It's scary. When will it stop? The arms dealers must be doing well with all these countries plagued by wars, rebellions, and dictatorships."

"You're quite right, darling. They're poisoning our lives. Today Julien only came for a little bit. He brought me some peaches, and we cooked them right away, but he left without getting a chance to taste them because of the machine-gun fire."

"I could tell from the garden! That smell makes you want to dig right in!"

"The peaches are delicious!" Mika heads to the storeroom for a snack.

We share some of the delicious jam, a moment of tender complicity in the intoxicating scent of the fleshy, juicy fruit that Mika explains was picked in the mountains. They grow in Kenscoff and Furcy, where the temperature is just right. We chat about this and that; Mika tells me about her childhood with Clarisse, who had a quick tongue, and who liked to climb trees and scale fences.

She goes to bed early, but later in the evening, I see a light under her door, and I knock. She is sitting up against her pillows, reading.

Her nightgown is lilac, her favourite colour, and her face is serene despite the constant shooting and the devils' racket up the road.

"They said on the news that gangs armed with picks and hammers destroyed three former ministers' homes, each one a palace. The retaliation won't be long. They're targeting the kids from the slums at the bottom of the hill. They're reckless, as you must have realized by now; they're not afraid of anything. I don't need to tell you again not to get too involved with them."

"It's too bad everything is being wrecked like this."

"It is. Those mansions, which were purchased on the backs of the poor, could have been used to set up schools, community halls, daycares. There's so much frustration, so much built-up resentment that people become blind. Smashing everything seems like the only way. Frankly, Junon, I'm fed up."

I wish I could say something to comfort her, but I don't know what. I pick up the book she's reading, by an author I don't know. Doris Lessing.

"It's from a series she wrote, *Children of Violence*." The title catches my attention. "It's largely autobiographical, a story of struggle against oppression, against the stifling moral and social constraints in South Africa when it was crippled by apartheid," Mika explains enthusiastically. "Lessing also talks about the political commitment that shaped her writing. Here, take it, I'm giving it to you."

"Are you sure?"

"I've read it many times," she reassures me. "There are some books I like to reread, often several times, because once we are rid of the idealized enchantment of youth, our eyes see things differently. Reading, like pleasure, improves with time."

"I'd like to know when you sleep! Your light is almost always on. Do you read all the time?"

"I sleep very little, it's true. Who knows," she laughs, "maybe I've learned to be wary of sleep too!"

Mika still laughs a lot, whole-heartedly. She often pokes fun at herself and at this country that she says has fallen on its head, at Clarisse and her antics—Clarisse, who's having a hard time getting old, Mika says. She ran away to in Mexico two years ago and has an unparalleled devotion to Frida Khalo and Diego Rivera.

"We try to keep in touch regularly. To be honest, with what's been going on, it's a relief that she's not here."

"What do you mean she's having a hard time getting old?"

"Well, after a lifetime of rejection, she took a lover half her age."

"What does it matter? Though do you think tía Clarisse would have wanted to get married?"

"The very word drove her crazy. She was always afraid of men, afraid of what they represent. She was in constant conflict with Papa about it. Our father was a caricature of conformity, and he never quite got over the fact that heaven only sent him daughters. I remember one particularly memorable argument between him and Clarisse: he was obsessed that Clarisse was still unmarried, he said it wasn't normal. Imagine: one day he decided to invite one of his acquaintances over, a doctor, which only showed how little he knew his daughter. For him, that man was a beacon! Clarisse mocked him: *How is it possible that nitwit can only talk about his work?*"

Mika tells me her life story, the family stories, as if they were straight out of the books she reads to forget the tragedy of existence. I take the opportunity to ask her if she and Banuteau are lovers. With a touch of malice, she answers that I am a fouyapòt. "Nosy; you want to know everything, you want to know too much," she says, pretending to go back to reading. I play innocent: I would like to get to know her better, that's all, and I can sense that she wants to tell me more. So I sit at the foot of her bed to hear a new story.

"Julien Banuteau is a very sleek, handsome man," Mika starts, then stops, no doubt wondering where to begin.

I'm not sure what she's talking about, but the word sleek makes me think of a racehorse. I don't want to rush her. I wait. She glances at the window.

"The day Banuteau snuck into my life, I thanked heaven for sending him to me. I was so grateful to have met this man, a true companion."

She winks at me. Shall I go make some tea, I ask her, risking the interruption. I rush to prepare two cups of verbena, her favourite herbal tea. I see Banuteau at the same time every day. He is so polite it's touching, at a time when everything is so ugly and rude. The day I arrived, I saw him through the bay window, striding up, smoothing his moustache as if he were going on a date. He reminds me of a tango dancer. He slips in quietly through the door left ajar, as if he were afraid he might not be allowed in. He always gives Mika a huge smile before taking her face in his hands and kissing her forehead. He looks like an eagle, on the lookout. I like him. *There aren't many people like your grandmother left*, he said when Mika introduced us.

Two days ago, the two of them were hiding in the living room because the pungent waft of smoke from the burning tires made it impossible to sit outside. They were drowsy, holding hands: Mika in an orangey-pink crepe de Chine dress with a lace collar, and him in his old, worn jacket over a stiff-collared shirt. They make vague pronouncements about the country heading who knows where, about what's happening in the world, as if they were already outside of time.

"You can imagine that, when I met him, at almost sixty, and with the baggage I have, I had given up any wish for a lover, a companion, a friend by my side. That's what he means to me."

"That's a lot."

"Above all, he is a great, great friend."

"It's a bit complicated, isn't it, abuelita?"

"Meaningful relationships help us live. A mutual friendship can make you want to share, to give the other person all we can, and not just to take from them."

"That kind of friendship means you have to be very human. It's about generosity, huge generosity."

"You're right. Yes, Banuteau offered me his friendship unconditionally, and I offered him mine. Friendship alone makes it possible to give yourself physically too, without holding back. That's what he and I have, true, utter total friendship that doesn't exclude physical love. It makes everything possible, it draws us toward each other, inside each other. It doesn't exclude sensuality, it enhances it. And it is intelligent, generous, sublime."

"Your relationship with Banuteau is all that?"

"All that and more. Banuteau is the one who showed me that it was possible for friendship, tenderness, and desire to coexist. His friendship revived my soul."

"Do you regret not having met him before? I mean before Charlot?"

"I am always in the present moment, Junon, that's what life has taught me. Bé was like that too. That was her legacy."

Mika pauses, lost in a pleasant memory. She smiles.

"Banuteau and I exchanged magazines, books, our views on international news, we discussed literature and politics. Then, one day, he had an envelope delivered, with an invitation to come and see a plant at his house."

"A plant?"

"That's right! A night-blooming cereus. It's a cactus, an odd plant—or, no, an extraordinary plant. It grows as it pleases and blooms once a year. The flower opens at night and dies the next day. When a cereus blooms it's so spectacular that some gardeners organize parties, like a birthday party, when it's about to flower. Since then, every year we celebrate the arrival of the flower and our meeting."

"Because that evening he…propositioned you?"

"We spent that night chatting in front of the plant that was about to wither and die the next day. And in the morning, while he was pouring me coffee, he leaned toward me and kissed me on the forehead. Apart from Bé and probably Mama, no one in the world has ever shown me such tenderness."

"But what happened next?"

"Since you won't leave me alone…I'll tell you."

I'm nestled into the pillows and now nothing else matters, not the men and the madness pouring into the city streets, not the fever that put me on a plane to throw me into this devastation. All that exists in the world are two women and a love story. Mika's voice is a lullaby.

"Right away I felt a tingling in my hair. I started to shake, I couldn't breathe. I ran to the window and he followed. I was on my guard, but all of a sudden the room started to sway and without really understanding how, with a single impulse, we found ourselves in each other's arms, kissing as if the world was going to end. How many years of desire, of the absence of pleasure, were released in those sighs, as we lost ourselves? That day, that day, I swear to you, my Junon, I prayed to heaven, I was so grateful that I could live that. That prayer was my triumph over the fear that was trying to corner me—the sly concern about what the herd would whisper, what people would think. I saw it, and, furious with myself, I started to fight it. And I savoured the embrace all the more. When Julien began to shout his pleasure, I panicked. I had never heard anyone climax like that before. I looked at him: he could see nothing, his eyes were full of tears."

LOVE, RELICS, AND PHILOSOPHY

THE NEXT MORNING, I WATCH MIKA. She's been up since dawn shuffling papers in cardboard boxes, on shelves, and in that huge mahogany cabinet she calls her shield. She destroys a lot, sets some aside for Soli and my aunts, some for uncle Félix. She'll probably mail them. I see her sorting heaps of old newspapers, postcards, photos—there are a tonne. Two large brown envelopes marked with the letter J are set aside. I'm curious to know what all the fuss is about. I don't dare ask her. Does she know something, is the country going under? Is Mika putting things in order before the fall?

It's been two weeks since I got here. The streets are so busy today that I'd rather not go out. Machine-gun fire kept us up all night. Clouds of blackish smoke from the burning tires smudge the horizon. It's barely light out. From the road we hear shouts and screams on the wind, rushing into the house even though the shutters are closed. We spend the morning in Mika's study, which looks like it's been closed up for years. It's still welcoming; there are pictures of her children at various ages, some framed and others tacked on the wall, and paintings by Clarisse and Soledad. I'm happy to recognize myself in the mosaic, a collection of faces reminding me that there are languages other than violence. There is the unconditional love of a formidable woman, Mika Pelrin, the care of my aunts Sonia and Maria, the love of María Luz. In a corner of the room, on a console table, more photos: Bé, Jeanne and Gertrude, my great-grandmother, Mika's mother. As I've been doing since I came here, I stand for a long time and look at these women, lined up there, each one in her frame. Take a break, I tell Mika, stop for a while, for a coffee. There are two metal rocking chairs. On each one there's a pile of shawls, which Mika picks up so we can sit.

"Those were Bé and Jeanne's chairs," Mika explains.

There are two magnificent flamenco mantóns brought back from Spain. Mika unfolds them to show me, smelling them, burying her face in the fabric.

"This room is like a sanctuary for you, isn't it?"

"It is a little like that."

As she speaks, Mika picks up an old tin from a corner of the table. She opens it and starts to sort the contents: safety pins, needles, mother-of-pearl buttons, thimbles.

"A sewing box is a repository for secrets," she says. "This one belonged to Mama Gertrude."

Her voice is thick, and the emotion in the room is palpable, as if there were another person here with us.

"I often feel them, their presence, so close it's stunning."

Our coffee has gone cold, but we drink it all the same, not wanting to break the spell. Time stretches out and we hold on to the happiness of being together. I gesture to the photos on the console.

"Do you ever talk to them?"

"Of course I talk to them! I wouldn't have survived without them. Wherever they are, they must be discouraged to see that this nightmare is far from over. Surely Bé is happy that I'm still standing. This used to be my study, but now, as you say, it's become a sanctuary. It's ironic, though, because it was once my prison. This was where I lived out my agony the nights before January 5, 1958. The presence of these women in this place gives me back some of my dignity. They make up for the lost words: I no longer write, but I talk to them, I tell them everything. It's important to me. When things go wrong, I know they're there. All I have to do is close my eyes, take a breath, and I can hear them. Our conversations give me strength, a primordial, fundamental life force. When I falter, they are the glue that allows me to put the pieces back together."

"Some people believe that the dead return to visit them."

"I am one of those people. And I assure you, I can hear their voices, Bé's voice especially, her radiant laughter."

"You can you hear their voices?"

"Of course."

"And you're not afraid?"

"It's the living we should be afraid of, my dear. Besides, I've been living with ghosts for so long. My mother's has been with me since I was five years old. I've always had long conversations with her. I remember Papa used to call me all kinds of names: he said I was crazy. Sometimes I still call her up when things get hard: *Listen, Mama Gertrude*, I say to her, *since the dead have powers, do whatever you can to get me out of this mess*."

Mika's face grows serious. She's just having fun, trying to scare me. But it's unnerving, and I don't know what to say. The idea of being in a house with ghosts walking around doesn't sound like fun to me at all.

"I know when they come," Mika says suddenly.

"When they come? Come where?"

Mika, still serious, stares at the front door.

"Sometimes," she says, "the door opens and then closes again without a sound. There's a draft and I know they're here. They enter the house with a kind of hot breath, like steam that rushes in with them. I hear them laughing, you know, a muffled laughter as if they were trying to not take up too much space. Once, not long ago, I heard Bé, that inimitable laugh of hers. And I could hear things moving in the tin. I thought Bé must be rummaging through the sewing box. I waited until she was gone, and then I opened the tin and I saw why she'd been laughing."

While she's talking, Mika opens the box and pulls out a pair of silver pince-nez. She bursts out laughing.

"This was one of Bé's trophies!"

"Trophies?"

"That man she married—it's funny, I don't even remember his name—he couldn't see anything."

Mika blows her nose and laughs again.

"He was always squinting, and he had all kinds of devices like this. To punish him, the day Bé left she took all his eyeglasses with her. Tante Jeanne nicknamed her Béatrice la Terreur."

"But why did she keep this one?"

"For one of her shows, no doubt," Mika replies, laughing again. "Bé knew how to have fun. She used to put on whole productions, complete with sets and costumes. She was both actress and audience. These rituals, she explained—and I quote—revivified her. Her favourite performances were those she referred to as burials for the harmful and useless. The goal was to get rid of things, thoughts, or circumstances—people, really—that she didn't want in her life. I would see her write all over huge sheets of kraft paper, covering them with her looping scrawl, and then meticulously rip them up and burn them in a steel canister."

"What was she writing?"

"A situation, an argument, something that was bothering her. She would write it all out in painstaking detail, then burn the paper and bury the ashes."

I'm shaking with laughter too, I can't help it.

"You haven't heard the best part," Mika breaks in as I laugh even harder. "Sometimes, when she felt like it, she would go dance on the ash-filled pit. Once she urinated on the pit. That was her ex-husband's funeral."

"Don't tell me she went to the funeral and then…"

"No," Mika says, "you don't understand. Early one morning, Bé got up and decided that he was dead to her and had to be buried. She cut up lots of photographs of him into tiny pieces and burned them, along with all their documents—marriage certificates, birth certificates, lots of other things. All dressed in white, like a Vodou priestess, she dug the hole herself and filled up the pit. Back then, Bé used to wear lots of bracelets, like Clarisse. When we looked outside, there was our Bé, dancing on the pit to the beat of her own music. She was very tall, so you can imagine it was quite a spectacle.

And all of a sudden, she hitched up her skirt and squatted, and we heard her cackling, *Drink up, hellion!*"

———◆———

Around five o'clock, we walk over to Banuteau's, who's invited us for dinner. The house looks like its owner, old-fashioned but neat. Even the brick of the patio and the layer of green moss seem to fit somehow. The house is built on a small rise, and a lush garden spreads out below. The air is heavy, charged, full of leaden clouds. Our evening, on the other hand, promises to be rather pleasant. Between delicious avocado and smoked salmon hors d'oeuvres, our gracious host shows me his imposing library. Most of the books have travelled around the world with him, first across Europe—France, then Switzerland where Banuteau studied engineering and architecture at the University of Geneva. He got his degree in architecture, then decided to study ancient languages and philosophy. Banuteau is indefatigable. He tells me about the Africa he knew, of all those newly independent states—Senegal, where he lived for several years, Congo, Guinea, Benin. Every place he travelled through, he says, had come through the brutality of colonial possession only to sink into the bloodbath of authoritarian regimes and tribal or ethnic struggles.

He entertains us, this elegant, handsome man, he fills our glasses ceremoniously, glides around us on his terrace, which is an oasis screened in by multicoloured bougainvillea. I am captivated by his supple movements—he must do yoga—but I've lost interest in his chatter. All the talking and twirling around is making me dizzy. For a long time I stare at his beige loafers with their soft, glossy leather and I understand that the weather at Banuteau's is not at all the same as the weather outside, beyond the fence that separates his property from the road.

This country contains two countries, two different times. My thoughts jump to Gabriel and his friends, locked in a time so far from any humanity, and Banuteau's French pinot, so fresh and so delicious, burns my throat. I suggest we go out to the garden. Mika and Banuteau exchange a complicit, embarrassed look when I ask them to introduce me to the cereus. Mika starts to flip through a magazine lying around on a pedestal table, while Julien Banuteau, delighted, precedes me out to his orchard.

"I planted everything myself," he explains proudly, striding around. "When I moved in, there was only a little patch of land covered in chickweed. Doesn't love work wonders? All I had to do was love this land, and see how it rewards me."

I admire his trees—oranges, avocados, papaya. I marvel at the lavish jacarandas, the pink and white oleander. Banuteau deplores what he calls man's sad divorce from the natural world; he can only live surrounded by plants, he says. We walk around the house to find Mika and enter through a veranda on the east side. That's where I discover that plant, the night-blooming cereus Mika told me about. With its long branches lolling here and there, it's all I can look at. It's such a unique plant, and I stop to stare at it. "My lucky plant," Banuteau says to himself.

He used to be a professor of Greek and philosophy, and after dinner we chat about this and that. Banuteau is of the opinion that we should reconsider the democratic model we want to impose on the world. Sovereignty, he explains, does not come from the people themselves. After a while, I'm only half-listening. I notice that he calls his old maid, Lina, over and over. Every time, she climbs the stairs, out of breath, running up to bring him a glass of water for his pills, then his scarf because he doesn't want to catch a cold, and I don't know what else. This refined man is a product of the very society he so loftily condemns. It was Lina who cooked the meal, who served it and then cleared the table. When I offer to help, Banuteau lifts his hand to stop me. I'm on the verge of losing it.

"How many years has Lina been serving you from morning to night, monsieur Banuteau?"

He looks at me, taken aback, and sputters something unintelligible. "I don't know anymore," I hear him mumble. Embarrassed, Mika comes to her friend's rescue. His servant has pretty enviable working conditions, she says.

"I even send her to the doctor regularly," Banuteau adds, braced by Mika's support.

"In a true democracy that provides equal opportunities for everyone, shouldn't this woman also be able to rest, at her age?"

Instead of answering me, this distinguished man with the neat moustache motions that I should lower my voice; Lina could hear us. He nods darkly, and Mika swaddles herself tighter in her shawl as if to protect herself. The seconds inch along. It has started to rain. The silence between us is so thick I can hear the raindrops on the slabs outside. Mika coughs loudly and Banuteau rushes out of the room. He is going to water the plants, he announces; it's been so hot. "What an interesting idea, watering plants in the rain," I say to Mika, sourly. In her face I see a hardness I've never seen before.

"You know, abuelita, his attitude toward Lina is unacceptable."

Her lips pursed, she still doesn't respond. For a long time, I am silent. Sitting before me in a rattan armchair, my grandmother tries to remain calm, though I can tell by the tiny, involuntary tightening of her face that she is trying to contain her temper.

I keep pushing: "Weren't you the first who taught me to refuse silence?"

To put an end to the ordeal, Mika decides it's best to go home. We say good night to Banuteau, who has come back from watering his plants, and we leave.

Mika walks out in front of me, chest out and chin jutting, whereas usually she likes to hold my arm. I'm disappointed, but I match her pace, and a thousand questions jostle inside me. It's true that with my grandmother I feel loved and understood, I'm less introverted, less aggressive, more outgoing. Mika gives me confidence in myself; should I have been more respectful with Banuteau because of her, I wonder? But then again, shouldn't she show some solidarity with that woman?

AS THE VOICELESS CRY

DAWN BREAKS, SULLEN. Mika and I have coffee quietly and then settle down in the living room, each reading a book, like a contest to see who will pout the longest. The sun barely manages to shine. Slowly, between sadness and disappointment, the hours pass. The morning promises to be a long one. I go out on the terrace to smoke a cigarette, and am greeted by a worrisome din floating up from the bottom of the hill. An invisible border has been breached, and a howl, belching from the bowels of the earth, surges up to us. Mika runs out. Her eyes wide with fright, she gathers her shawl, falters. I hold her back, take her arm. We hurry back in the house and close the door, but the voices follow us inside.

Mika is on the alert. "Listen! Listen close, I hear women screaming. The voice of death, that's what it is." I get dressed quickly and pace back and forth while I wait for Mika, who's decided to come with me—she wants to be with me to protect me, but it's a peace offering, too. It's impossible to keep the distance that set in between us after what happened last night. Neither of us can hold a grudge, and we can't stand to be cut off from life as it cries out for help.

Other people come running, some crashing through the brambles and thickets that line the road while others lurch around, their arms stretched out in front of them.

I'd love to bolt downhill, but I have to keep pace with Mika. I think about Gabriel and my knees buckle—his recklessness, and the raid they were planning in La Plaine.

How many of us are running like this, beckoned by the call of death? Curious people passing by and friends and relatives pop up all over, yanked out of bed by the noise. It's not even screams. As Mika said, it's the voice of death coming up the road from the basins and the ravines and it drags us down to the welter of shacks below.

The wailing swells, stronger than anything, from the mouths of mothers and fathers who have lost children in yet another massacre. The mutilated bodies of several young people have just been found in an old sand quarry.

The shouts lead us to Mélanie's house. She is screaming and writhing in the dust. Her two boys are among the victims, and Gabriel too. Other women are clinging to trees so they don't fall and die on the spot, overcome. The men rock on their heels, bawling, clutching their heads in their hands as if they were about to be torn off.

Mélanie has gone completely mad: she gets up and runs inside to grab a knife. Lurching like a drunk, she staggers to a pen where two pigs huddle, growling. She swirls in the dust, tearing at her clothes. It takes four men to restrain her. We can hear her screaming that all she can do now is die, sacrificed like a sow: "That's all we are, look at what they've done with our children. They've bled them like pigs."

Later, Banuteau calls one of his friends' doctors to get some sedatives. I'm going to go to the wake with him tonight. Mika isn't up to it.

"When I came to live in this neighbourhood," she tells me, "Mélanie was just a girl, so pretty, happy, helpful. Life took a toll on her; it broke her."

Mika has known Mélanie for at least twenty-five years. She saw the boys born and watched them grow. Mélanie called her two sons her pòtòtrezò: they were her strength and her treasures.

Locked up in her study, Mika cries all afternoon in front of the photos of Bé, Jeanne, and her mother Gertrude, her three amazons, powerless.

"If the dead had any power at all, we would have long since been rid of that filth," she sniffles. "Like many people, you probably believe that Saint Mika has forgotten and forgiven everything," she snaps. "But if you do, you're making a big mistake, child. You can't forgive when the executioner feels there's nothing to forgive. I may have put the hatred and resentment to sleep, but I've forgotten nothing, absolutely nothing. Believe me, I will hate them until the day I die for the way they stripped me naked, they condemned me, for the rest of my life. I have never stopped looking for a place to hide. My silence? My silence was to try to hold on to what little dignity they left me. With all my soul, I have always wanted to take revenge on those bastards!"

I'm dumbfounded, breathless. This is the first time I've heard Mika say anything like this.

◆

On the day of the funeral, soldiers parade through the neighbourhood. They strut, they tear around, tires squealing, throwing up thick clouds of grey dust. This could all end in riots and shooting, Mika and Banuteau predict, but I've decided that I have to go to the funeral, whatever the cost. Banuteau, despite his reluctance, is coming with me.

The church is full to bursting, and more people are gathered in the square and the surrounding streets. On one side, the provocation: motorbikes backfiring, blue and red uniforms, rifles. On the other side, the crowd: women dressed in white, scarves tied around their heads and at the waist, moaning and keening, and men who know they have no choice but to stand up and keep going. I didn't know all of them were going to be sung to rest at the same time.

"This is too much," I whisper to Banuteau, who stands stiffly, struck by the courage of all these people ground down without mercy. I hold on to his arm, and a slight tremor goes through him. From time to time he gives me a little squeeze with his other hand, as if to say, *I'm here, I'm with you. I'm at your side, and I am with them, too. Trust me.*

Cries, at first solitary and plaintive, begin to rise up from everywhere in the aisles as the priest gives his homily, speaking of the priceless gift of children—"the children that God has given us and that he takes back from us." From the back of the nave, a voice shouts out, *se pa Bondye, se asasen!* It's not God at all, it is assassins: the voices know, and they climb to a crescendo, superhuman and terrifying, as the women's choir sings a farewell song that everyone takes up in unison.

Banuteau and I don't go to the cemetery. The road is long and the sun is already very hot. We shuffle back to the house where Mika awaits, her face undone by sadness. We nibble at a salad and some cold chicken. We eat in silence, as if we accept these calamities, which we warily call misfortune; we eat, feeling small and confined in this life. We eat little, and Mika and Banuteau take refuge in the living room to hold hands and convince each other that they are alive. I go vomit up my lunch, like I'm throwing up my insides, but my distress and my hunger for revenge remains, like a terrible child growing inside me, a child who will destroy my life the day it makes its voice heard, I know it.

That afternoon, I finally grab the two large brown envelopes that have been on Mika's desk since my arrival. I've noticed that she tends to move them around, putting them on the armchair and then back on the table. I suspect she's a bit hesitant. Is she afraid of my reaction? Or does she hope that I'll be too curious and open them? What she doesn't know is that I already know what's in them.

Copies of these documents are kept at Soledad's. My quest has lasted almost twenty years—my need to dive into the past to try to understand Soli, to find the source of her sorrow and her immutable outrage, has led me to open many drawers. I've searched everywhere, and I found press clippings about the odious crime of January 5, 1958. I cross-checked them, found the names, drew conclusions. But in these envelopes, for the first time, I see photos, carefully labelled. On the back of each one, Mika has written identifying details, and the role each person played.

◆

I realized very quickly that there was no way I could get access even to dusty, yellowed registers, or to the archives of the police or any ministry. What would have been the point, anyway? I walked through the streets, trying to talk to people, who were frightened by my audacity and basically ran away. There would be no old men or griots on my path whom I could ask about this story, which seemed to never have happened. So despite my reluctance, I decided to go to the makout themselves. I was impressed at how easily my *El País* press pass opened the palace doors for me; my exotic accent and good-girl face did the rest. All the smug, potbellied men I met had something to say about the nascent democracy in this country, a democracy of which they were the architects, naturally. They invited me to eat with them, tried to seduce me. I choked back my aversion and politely declined or accepted, depending on each man's importance. I continued my search, and finally learned that the one I wanted most of all was hiding in the southeast, in the town of Marigot.

I gleaned this information from an old drunkard, who would have been pathetic if he hadn't had so much blood on his hands. The man, whose name is Romain, boasted that he had been part of the first generation—the real ones, he claimed with pride. He introduced himself as a retired major—"always at the service of my country!"—and proudly displayed his military badge and the weapon he carried. Over the course of our interview, on the terrace of a pizzeria in Pétion-Ville, I finally found out the man's exact address. During that meeting, there was some nameless unease among the people at the table. Did they imagine I was a prostitute ready to surrender to this piece of shit in exchange for a meal? Was it fear? Several clients froze when Romain appeared. The hubbub of voices subsided suddenly, and the waiter fell over himself in his eagerness to rush to our table.

I can still hear his words, that beast, nostalgic for the years when Papa Dòk was at the helm: "We were a crack team, I tell you. The country was running like clockwork. We didn't tolerate mistakes. It was me, and Gracia, Barbot, Désir, Maître, and Borges, and others, too, because it was no small task. Some of them have crossed over to heavenly shores, but their souls remain at our side. Désir is my neighbour, if you want to meet him, it's no problem, we both live in Morne Cabrit. As for Benjamin, he retired to Marigot, on a property in Les Orangers. Impasse des Petits Oiseaux, 24. I often spend weekends with him, the beach is close by. He is still as cool as ever. He was never very talkative, and has remained the same except about two years ago he had some minor health problems. He had a weakness for beautiful women, that was his only flaw."

MARIGOT, A SHROUD FOR A CAUL

MIKA TAUGHT HER that there are many kinds of words. Some words can open doors and windows, and even bring down barricades. Others are used to solve riddles, while others make our soul sing. Junon didn't remember the words to use to describe her state of mind during those early days of March. What she did know was that after spending more than a month in the country, that land to which she was bound by both love and hate—a bond of suffering, terrible, fleeting things—she was about to unfurl a shroud she had been patiently weaving for years. Shroud: that was the only word that came to mind. *I'm going to open myself up to the world*, she thought to herself, *open and clear-eyed*. How many years does it take for the dust to settle, for the hands of time to undo what was done? She had been waiting all those years to be born at last.

Junon had insisted on cooking supper the night before she left, to say goodbye to Mika and Banuteau. It was better to stay in a hotel tonight, she explained, to avoid traffic jams and other problems on the way to the airport. Would she see Mika again? Quite possibly this was the last time: her grandmother was almost eighty. Junon had the peculiar impression that Mika was relieved to see her go. The loathing that rooted and grew in Junon's heart like a tree spreading wide its branches cast icy shadows over Mika's world.

In the afternoon, she packed up a small car she'd rented under a fake name. In less than an hour, she was ready. While she was packing, she phoned Soli and then María Luz. Both women chided her for not having called, and she reassured them as best she could.

The day before, Junon had visited the area for the second time. She'd left the car in a safe place on the road to Kenscoff and taken a camionette that dropped her off at the main road, near the street leading to the Impasse des Petits Oiseaux. She had spent the afternoon in the neighbourhood, first on the empty beach, then strolling here and there to get a feel for the place. There were few people on this road, and almost no houses. Colonies of green lizards swarmed in the grass, bright as lightning.

Now the weather was overcast, but she liked the gloom of the twilight, the wind's lashing gone quiet and the trees returning to their peaceful posture as the sun got lost in the distance. In the dim, waning day, everything has become pale and icy. She felt cold, because of the breeze off the sea but also because of the fatigue and emotion of the last few days. She had wanted to go off the main road, which was rutted and still today crowded with vans and trucks careening around—big Jeeps overflowing with soldiers, ordinary vans kitted out as tanks. Although many weeks had passed since their leader's departure, these manoeuvres were still going on, to try to intimidate people, to get them to stop settling scores with the makout. Within half an hour, she calculated, she would be at her destination. She found the small side road easily and parked the car out of sight among the trees.

―――――◆―――――

The narrow path was hard to walk on, a dark, muddy strip of land that cut through the brush. Her footsteps sank into soil thick with clay, which made her progress difficult. Branches swept across the path and thorns scratched her face, but she hardly felt a thing. Bottomless calm. Nothing but her footsteps sucking in the muck. The wind was up, and carried the vague scents of plants she couldn't recognize. The house wasn't far from the beach, and she was crouched behind a high dune. She moved her fingers, which were going numb. Twenty minutes: the man at the pizzeria had told her that he usually went to bed at seven, after the maid who served him his supper had left.

Sheltered and trusting her lucky star, which had led her by the hand and guided her steps, she waited there, at peace, and she looked back on her life. Something insistent held her by the throat, and she told herself that her youth was over now. Isn't that how it goes, when the cold takes over, leaves us with a landscape of wounds, shame, and resentment? A rabid cloud closed around her heart. She was ready to face hell, she said to herself, she would do anything to give this story a voice. The moment of reckoning had come.

The owner seemed intent on discretion: the house was built at the end of a huge courtyard, with bushy camellia hedges stretching out on either side of walls that obstructed the view. The house was sturdy, reminiscent of the colonial homes in parts of the United States. A coffee-coloured resin covered the columns of the huge verandah. The garden was a dark tangle. Dwarf palms, coconut palms, banana trees, and other plants whispered, muffled in the night.

She hadn't expected the gate to be closed, but it was chained and padlocked tight. Junon didn't insist and went around the concrete wall, which thankfully hadn't been bristled with shards. She climbed it on a side of the house where there were no doors or windows. Jumping down, she landed on a thick carpet of damp leaves and moss, just as she heard the voices.

"There's no need to ask him the same question. They're all liars. He'll just keep lying."

It sounded like an older man, but still Junon thought of Gabriel. The same fire, the same ardour. Could it be that this raid, as he and his group called their attacks on the butchers' dens, had been planned before his death? She had told him everything she knew... hadn't she? Gabriel, she recalled, said he knew everything about the man from Marigot: "He's on our list, I have his file," he'd said harshly.

"Who sent you?" someone barked.

It had to be Astrel Benjamin, the man she had come to meet.

"Pass me the gun so I can answer him!" another voice ordered.

"We've already wasted far too much time with this motherfucker."

"Not yet, not so fast," another voice replied. "Monsieur Benjamin," he went on, "we're going to tell you why we're here. As for who sent us, what an impertinent question. Did you know that there are men—flunkies, really—who are sent to women's homes in the dead of night to rape and assault them? That's not us. We're not here on the orders of any jackboot regime, or summoned by some evil force. We have come of our own free will. We are here because of a sense of duty—to hold you to account. We've come for you, monsieur Benjamin!"

Whoever had spoken was pacing back and forth. From her position in the bushes, Junon could hear his footsteps. He seemed like the leader, and asked one of the others to read Benjamin's indictment. At the same time, Junon heard an irritated grunt, followed by a sharp jerk and a lingering whine. A window opened, and Junon once again heard the same voice.

"Throw those canes out the window!" Something landed in the camellias with a thud.

"They say you've had health problems. I guess you can't even move around without your walking stick, unless you throw yourself to the ground and crawl. And that would be rather risky, and useless, especially, wouldn't you say?"

"Who are you? Where did you come from?"

Junon would have given anything to see his face, the face of the man who had just snarled like a beast cornered. No one bothered to answer him. Suddenly a thin voice—a young girl—piped up.

"Look at that bloated body, look at this animal! Who are we? You'll know soon enough. Where did we come from? From our mamas' wombs! We didn't come all the way out here to argue. We are here, in your hovel, only to uphold the principle of retribution. And in the name of that principle, you will die, by your own hand. If you refuse, simple: we'll set the house on fire, so you die anyway.

Unless you manage to get out, which is unlikely. Everything we need to start a fire is out on the verandah."

The man's breathing became laboured. Slowly, Junon moved a little closer to the door. The space between the hinges and the frame was just wide enough for her to glimpse a small room and a rattan armchair. A stocky man sat in the chair, folded up on himself. His forehead was bony, his hair sparse, and his eyes disappeared under bushy eyebrows. He was staring, bewildered, at two men and a girl.

"Are you afraid?" the girl asked him. "Are you hoping to make us cry? After such a long and illustrious career, after torturing, raping and murdering so many people, you expect me to believe that these two amateurs and a girl can scare you? Come on! I'm sure you'll be as brave as ever."

"But what atrocities are you talking about, madame?" the man blustered. "I have only served my country. I never overstepped, there was never any abuse. I only did my duty."

One of the men leapt at him as if to slap him. The girl caught his arm. Then she spit in the old man's face.

"Do excuse me," she snarled. "I grew up without a father to discipline me and I had a mother who was absent, bruised, and completely traumatized by rape—the rape I came from. Do you understand? She was raped one night by a son of a bitch, a hyena, who looked just like you. My poor mother did her best, but I'm afraid I don't have very good manners. When hyenas invaded the neighbourhood, they often raped all the girls in the same family. Do you understand, monsieur Benjamin?"

The girl was sobbing.

"My hatred is the weight of all these years of suffering, my mother's suffering and my own, the suffering that I lived through when every single day I had to face the revulsion of the woman who gave birth to me, her disgust. She was barely able to lay eyes on me, she couldn't take me in her arms, look at me, talk to me. I look so much like you."

Her voice faltered, but she went on.

"Those bushy eyebrows, those thick lips…I finally understand the extent of her sacrifice. More than anything else, it was her silence that killed me slowly. And you will pay for that silence, the silence against which she had no power, the silence that was her only lifeline. My mother was a wreck all her life; my mother, stripped of everything; my mother, irremediably mute."

Junon's limbs were trembling. How was it possible that this young woman was speaking her words, Junon's own life? The man tried to stand, as if on impulse. It was high time for her to leave, she told herself, but her legs were unsteady, and she didn't know if this was a dream or reality.

Robotically, she backed out to the road, to her car in the bushes. A huge moon suddenly appeared in the sky as if to show her the way. Now she was walking fast, very fast. Her feet barely touched the ground. How many of us are here in this country with our lives in tatters? She wanted more than anything to be sitting on the plane, and she thought of María Luz, her longing so sharp that she started to cry.

◆

In the house, the man was panting and flailing as if he were dancing in his chair. Because he was a coward, he continued to moan weakly. The girl thought he was drooling, and sneered in disgust before realizing that it was her own spittle dripping down to his mouth.

"Who are you," the man sniffed again, "to come and talk to me about justice?"

"Who's talking to you about justice? Have we even uttered the word? You don't know who I am, yet there must be so many women and children in this country, in this city, who dream of standing before you to do what I'm doing. Who I am really doesn't matter; I am one of many."

"Now," the younger of her two companions said, walking toward the man dumped into the armchair, "I am going to ask you a few questions, just as a formality. Answer simply with yes or no. Is your name Astrel Benjamin?"

"Yeah."

"Were you, on the night of January 5, 1958, a member of the death squad sent on the orders of François Duvalier to the home of the journalist Mika Pelrin, and the next day, to the home of the Jean-Baptiste girls, on Tirmasse?"

"I was there, but it wasn't me. That night there was Romain, Barbot, Maître, Désir, Ti Boulé, Gros Féfé, Gracia, André, Paul... Milice Midy, Bòs Pete, Zacharie Delva..."

"Basta!" the girl shouted.

"I don't know who else," he muttered. "I was an army officer, I was just obeying orders." The excuse rattled out in a single breath. "Actually, I think it was someone called Ti Boulé that night or Albert or maybe Pierre, I've forgotten, I don't know. It was so long ago."

"You were there but it wasn't you? It wasn't you, it was Pierre, Albert, Orcel, Tassy, it was Peter Rabbit, it was Jérôme, Décembre? Didn't you even boast, after it was done, that you'd eaten your fill?"

"They were Duvalier's orders," he protested again.

"So you committed these crimes and everything else that you're accused of only because it was your duty?"

The man said nothing more.

"Are you going to answer? Yes or no!?"

Terror blazed from his pupils like lightning bolts. He inhaled sharply and shivered.

"You're going to smoke, you're going to burn alive!" the girl screamed at him. "Imagine the fire rising from the floor, the flames licking your chair. It's wicker, isn't it? What a beautiful crest of sparks that will make. Then your legs, which you won't even be able to move. Picture the tap behind you in the kitchen, but you'll have no way to quench your thirst. And imagine your favourite weapon, between your bastard thighs, in pain, shrivelled and charred. What an end for the thing that's destroyed so many lives. That terrifying, fearsome weapon—nothing more than a dog turd in the fire! Come on, keep going: your heart, lungs, spleen, liver, crimping, dissolving, disappearing. And the raging flame climbing up to your face."

The man groaned again.

"That's enough, animal! No one is going to come to your rescue. You've done so much harm here, you've killed so many people, you've destroyed so many lives. Everyone hates you. They'll be happy to let you die! But we can avoid the fire; we can put the barrel of the gun in your mouth and you'll shoot yourself."

The girl motioned to one of the other two. One of them came up and leaned toward the man, who bucked. The chair gave way. The man tried to move his left hand to grasp the pistol with his deformed fingers, and was cuffed with the butt of the rifle. Desperate, he leapt, throwing himself at the table where an oil lamp glowed. They only had time to put a bullet in his foot before they left the scene.

They had strung dozens of coconuts together around the house with long strands of cotton and raffia. All the wicks came together in the same place, buried under a thin layer of straw on the highest mound of soil before the beach.

Inside, the man was shouting. The fire's fierce crackle could be heard from far away.

They only needed to set one or two wicks on fire, Gabriel had insisted, since they would all come together; the wind would take care of the rest. And that was what they did.

———◆———

When Junon's car reached the top of Morne La Vallée, at the junction that led to the border, she stopped. At the bottom of the hill she could see long plumes of smoke and enormous reddish tongues.

She closed her eyes for a moment, and a fairy-tale vision flashed before her eyes: women standing around a fire wearing long skirts lined with wide lace frills were dancing a fandango, their bracelets tinkling. She could hear the castanets. Down there, far down, the fire hissed. Like a greedy snake, it twined around the house.

Someday, on a day like today, Junon thought, *someday when my hair is white, I'll come back to dance and piss on those ashes.* She turned at the crossroads. *Right now, I'll just sit and watch as everything that's been burning inside me goes out.*

ACKNOWLEDGEMENTS

My sincere thanks to the Centre national du livre (CNL) and the Association Montargue in French Guiana, without whose financial support this book would nonetheless certainly have been written, but under much more difficult conditions.

To Line Colson at the Boutique d'Écriture de Montpellier, thank you for having given me the space to develop the first drafts of this book, for our discussions, and for your candour, which helped me get out of my comfort zone.

To Julianna Rimane and Denis Gerval at the Montargue Association in Kourou, your generous welcome and your dedication to literature and culture moved me immensely during my last writing trip to Guyana. Thank you for all your kindness.

To Rachel at Éditions du remue-ménage, you have supported me for twenty years, and I have benefited greatly from your rigour; thank you.

To Valérie Lefebvre-Faucher, thank you for your close and constructive reading and re-reading.

To my friend Clorinde Zéphir, thank you for being so generous and so present throughout the years when I was working on this novel.

To Didier C. for your support and kindness, a balm in hard times.

To all of my friends who carried this project with me, thank you for listening and for your encouragement.

Marie-Célie Agnant
Montréal, 2008
Montpellier, 2011–2012
Kourou, French Guiana, 2013
Montréal, 2015

TRANSLATOR'S NOTES

Excerpts from the following poems are evoked and cited in the book, in my translations: Guillaume Apollinaire's *Lettres à Lou* (page 38); Rainer Maria Rilke's "Das Stunden-Buch" (page 77); and Pablo Neruda's "Testamento de otoño" (page 95) and "Para subir al cielo" (page 101). Readers may also wish to consult the excellent translations of the foregoing by Martin Sorrell, Ralph Freedman, and Alastair Reid, respectively.

I would like to acknowledge the work of the late Luciana Ricciutelli, editor-in-chief at Inanna Publications for three decades, who sparked this translation but never got to see it through. Thanks to Renée Knapp at Inanna and Ashley Rayner at Inkwell's for shepherding the novel along, and to the Maison de la littérature and the Literary Translators' Association of Canada for a residency that made it possible for me to work with the author. My deepest thanks to Janice Flavien for her generous readings and discussions, to Louise Hill and Philippa Jabouin for proofreading so well and with such care and to Nadine Mondestin for her editorial eye, sharp and kind. And to Marie-Célie: chère amie, je suis choyée.

KG

ABOUT THE AUTHOR

Credit: Alain Lefort

A poet, short story writer, young adult fiction writer, storyteller, and novelist, Marie-Célie Agnant was born in Haiti and has lived in Québec since 1970. Many of her books evoke the hardships endured by women in the West Indies and the difficulty of legitimizing this part of history even today. Her work has been published in Québec, France, and Haiti, and translated into several languages.

Her novel *Le dot de Sara* (Remue-Ménage, 1995) was a finalist for the Desjardins prize, her collection of short stories *Le silence comme le sang* (Remue-Ménage, 1997) was a finalist for the Governor General's prize for fiction, and she has won the Prix Gros Sel for her children's book *La légende du poisson amoureux* (Mémoire d'encrier, 2003), the prose creation prize awarded by the SODEP for "Sofialorène, si loin de la délivrance," and the prestigious Prix Alain-Grandbois for her third collection of poems *Femmes des terres brûlées* (Éditions de la Pleine Lune, 2016).

ABOUT THE TRANSLATOR

Katia Grubisic is a writer, editor, and translator whose work has appeared in various Canadian and international publications including *The Walrus*, *The Fiddlehead*, *The Globe and Mail*, *Grain*, *The Spoon River Poetry Review*, and *Prairie Fire*. Her collection *What if red ran out* (Goose Lane Editions, 2008) was shortlisted for the A.M. Klein Prize for Poetry and won the 2009 Gerald Lampert award for best first book.

Her book translations include Louis Patrick Leroux's play *False Starts: A Subterfuge of Excellent Wit* (with Alexandre St-Laurent; Talonbooks, 2016), Martine Delvaux's *White Out* (LLP, 2018), Jeanne Painchaud's *ABCMTL* (ruelle, 2019), Stéphane Martelly's *Little Girl Gazelle* (ruelle, 2020), Ioana Georgescu's *Daughter of Here* (LLP, 2020), and Marie-Claire Blais's *Songs for Angel* (House of Anansi, 2021). Her translations of David Clerson's first novel, *Brothers* (QC Fiction, 2016), and of Alina Dumitrescu's *A Cemetery for Bees* (LLP, 2021) were shortlisted for the Governor General's Award for translation.